THE TAY IS WET

Spinning Yarns in Co Meath

ORIGINAL WRITING

© 2010 Ben Ryan

Front Cover by Sirocco Design Studio ph 086 8361982

978-1-907179-54-9

A CIP catalogue for this book is available from the National Library.

Published by Original Writing Ltd., Dublin, 2010.

Printed by Cahill Printers Limited, Dublin.

ACKNOWLEDGEMENTS

This writing project was made so much easier because of the wonderful encouragement of family and friends and to say I am grateful to all is an understatement.

Special thanks to Noel Friel, John McCullen and Paddy Gibney, who read initial drafts, for their valuable critiques. Also to Peter McCullen for a beautiful front cover design.

Sincere thanks to Original Writing duo, Steven Weekes for his layout and design skills and Garrett Bonner for managing and overseeing the project.

Most of all thanks to my own family and especially to my wife, Nuala, for her infinite patience and understanding while I was "writing" and for ensuring at all times that *the tay was wet*.

Ben Ryan, February, 2010

CONTENTS

Acknowledgements   *iii*

Preface   *vii*

Timmy and the Duke   I

A Mass for Billy the Kid   7

The Wedding Breakfast   11

The Black Pony   17

War and Peace   23

In the Back Row   31

Head or Harp?   37

Dressing Down   45

A Judge of Colour 51

The Singer, Not the Song 57

Arrival of the Queen of Sheba 63

Never Judge a Book 71

Holidays With Tay 77

Knit No More Mother Dear 83

Waiting for a Train 87

On the Other Foot 93

Glossary 98

Great romantic odes poets have set

Praising Beatrice and pert Juliet

Even Mozart ne'r made

Such a sweet serenade

As "come in, wipe your feet, the tay's wet."

PREFACE

The cinema and the dancehall played a significant part in providing, not only entertainment, but also some relief from the grinding and unending struggle to put bread on the tables of rural Ireland during the nineteen forties and fifties. Whistling and singing at work made mundane tasks seem lighter. Annual holidays became the norm. The general theme of the book is this bygone social scene of "pictures and dances" as recalled by the author and conveyed through the character, Timmy Deery, a simple man who makes us laugh but who also commands our respect for his innate good nature and decency.

Cinema was a social phenomenon not only in Ireland but in all countries whose ideology permitted its influence. Many of us who grew up in those times well remember when the main topic of conversation as we "drew" in the hay or "stucked" the corn was "what Judy Garland did last night in the pictures." Actors and actresses became real people to us. We knew them as neighbours and friends or if they were "baddies" as enemies who deserved their comeuppance.

I have tried, in this little book, to recall some of those events and to add whatever life the written word will allow so that, hopefully, the reader will have a pleasurable and rewarding experience.

Ben Ryan, February, 2010

To the memory of my sister, Theresa 'Tess' Carry, a supreme tea-maker, who passed away during the writing of this book.

At the weekend their hair they let down

All the country folk painted the town

And the Duke in his kilt

Sang a highlander's lilt

Mondays some had a hung-over frown

I

TIMMY AND THE DUKE

Ivor Nale, whistled "Over the Rainbow" as he worked to repair the door of the old cow-byre which had been damaged by an agitated cow the previous day. Ivor was a local handyman and was often called upon to carry out odd jobs for the Deery family. Inside the cow-byre Timmy Deery sang "I'll Be Seeing You" as he milked the remaining ten cows. Sonny Deery, Timmy's brother, quietly finished strigging the nervous cow in a nearby shed.

As Timmy's singing got louder, Ivor also increased the volume of his whistling. Soon the two were building up a cacophony of noise as one tried to drown out the other. Sonny's patience was wearing thin, as he was finding the cow, which had a sore elder, difficult to milk.

'Stop that infernal racket,' he roared.

At this the nervous cow lashed out with her back legs and overturned Sonny's bucket of milk. The only one to show approval at this calamity was the Deery cat, which always lurked around at milking time ready to lap up any milk that was spilt. When the cow calmed down Sonny read the riot act to the two jokers and then stomped back to resume his delicate task.

'He has no ear for music,' Timmy muttered, 'You know, Ivor, the great fire of Chicago started when a cow kicked over an oil lamp and set fire to the straw bedding.'

'Is that right?'

'Yes, it is, I saw it at the pictures.'

Timmy was an ardent cinema-goer. He would cycle the ten miles from the old stone farmhouse, where he lived with his brother, Sonny, and sister-in-law, Henrietta, and their three teenage children, to the town of Roggart, which boasted the only cinema in the county that showed the latest Hollywood films. My father knew him well as they were class-mates in primary school. An unusual incident with a pony took place one day at the school and both Timmy and my father were involved.

Timmy was now regarded as the local eccentric. This was not because he was still a care-free bachelor at forty years of age, but rather because of small mannerisms and idiosyncrasies which he exhibited. For instance he rubbed his hands together when he was excited. He did not drive a car, even though Sonny's old Hillman Minx would be available to him as the brothers got on well together. He did drive the old Fordson tractor, but only on the farm. He rode a green bicycle while everyone else's was black. His speech was slurred yet he could sing clearly and, in fact, was quite a good singer. He was not learned yet was an excellent hand-writer. Recently he had received a strange letter in the post and also had begun a new unconventional behaviour. Every Saturday morning he would get up an hour earlier than he usually did and ride off towards town on the green bicycle. He always returned home in time to start work on the farm as usual. If anybody questioned where he had been his family and friends simply said "He's in training for the Olympics." But Henrietta was walking past a hotel in Roggart one morning and noticed a green bicycle leaning against the hotel wall.

'That's odd,' she thought, but as she had an urgent doctor's appointment, she continued on her way and by evening had forgotten all about it.

The biggest night in Roggart was Saturday night. On this night a fleet of bicycles would sweep downhill towards the "Grand" cinema. Every active person, from sixteen to sixty, headed for town. They rode in groups of five or six together laughing and singing the latest songs from the radio. The girls would sing *She wears red feathers and a hula-hula skirt* or *Meet me in St Louis, Louis, meet me at the Fair.* Timmy was a strong cyclist and liked to imagine that he was riding to the Californian gold rush or that he was the Sheriff of Tombstone in pursuit of Jesse James and his gang. He would streak past the other cyclists while singing at the top of his voice *I'll be there, Mary Dear, I'll be there, when the fragrance of the rose fills the Air.*

One evening in early summer when the flight into Roggart was in full swing the cyclists were scattered off the road by a motor car which was being driven at speed and in an erratic manner.

'It's the Duke,' someone shouted, 'he's got himself a car.'

The Duke's real name was Donald Dunlase. He had come from Scotland when he was twelve years old to be reared by his aunt Matilda, a widow, who lived in a small well kept cottage at the end of Deery's lane. He was called "the Duke" locally because he always boasted that he was descended from "The Duke of Lammermoor," whom nobody in Roggart had ever heard of. He was a colourful character who sometimes wore a kilt and was considered by some to be acting above his station in life.

He could converse on any subject although he had left school at fourteen. He worked in the local hardware shop selling farming items but he had ambitions to achieve higher things. The car had been won by the Duke at a "Pitch and Toss" gambling session and there was much gossip and amusement when the Parish Priest used this as the subject of his anti-gambling Sunday sermon. This did not bother the Duke at all as he rarely attended church, a characteristic which did not exactly endear him to mothers who had daughters of marriageable age.

Getting a car had been a long held ambition of the Duke. He could not drive but was always prepared to take a chance and, with luck, attain some measure of success. On that first drive into Roggart the last cyclist he passed was Timmy Deery and as he passed he hooted the horn loudly and Timmy got such a fright that he fell off the bike and onto the grassy bank along the roadside. Timmy was not hurt but he had recognized the driver and promised himself he would get even. The Duke had parked the car right outside the cinema entrance and Timmy rubbed his hands with glee when he saw it. He gazed nonchalantly at the car and then, breaking an old used matchstick between his teeth, he walked around to the side which was next the road and quickly inserted this into one of the uncapped tyre valves. He then casually went in to see the film.

The Duke noticed the flat tyre as soon as he came out of the cinema.

'Blooming Lough Lomond, do ye ken that,' he said in his loud Scottish accent. Then turning to a small group of tittering local youths he said, 'Here, laddies, did ye see anyone interferin' wih ma car tyres?'

The youths all shook their heads but one of the older and cheekier of them spoke up.

'I saw someone at your wheels, mister.'

'Did ye now laddie and what were they doing?'

'They were washing them.'

'Wha' ye mean, what did they look like?'

'They were two dogs, mister.'

The outbreak of laughter caused by this remark did not last very long. The Duke, who had a tall intimidating presence, was not likely to be deterred by a bunch of young smart aleks.

'So, twa dogs was it? Do any of you laddies want to earn some hard cash?'

The Duke took out a handful of silver which made the young lads gasp.

'Yeah,' 'please,' 'me,' 'I do.'

They all swarmed forward and under the directions of the resolute, but genial, Scotsman the wheel was soon changed. He then jumped into the driving seat, wound down the window and, throwing a handful of coins out, drove away in a cloud of exhaust smoke. He smiled as he observed the scrimmage over the coins in his back view mirror. The youths rushed into the small general store which was still open to spend their new-found wealth but they were not smiling when they handed over the coins to pay and the shopkeeper shook his head.

'What's this?' He glared at the coins.

'These are some kind of Scottish shillings. I can't take this money. It's no good to me. The bank would not accept this.'

The chastened youngsters were disappointed but putting on a brave face they resumed their usual pursuits. Meanwhile the Duke also learned a lesson that night and, also, he never did find out who let the air out of his tyre.

Soon after he got the car the Duke started going out with a girl who lived forty miles away. It was said that she was a wealthy heiress and his neighbours thought that this would end in tears when she discovered that he had no property or wealth. One weekend the Duke brought the girl to a local dance and showed her around the biggest farm in the parish, intimating that he was the owner. He brought her into the fine farmhouse for tea as he had arranged with the real owner, a bachelor friend, to lay on a swanky meal and the friend to serve them as if he was the butler.

'Oh, Donald,' she cooed, 'this is really the style.'

'Well, ma butler says, that's the style that Mary sat on.'

Soon after this the Duke and the girl got married and it was only then that they both discovered that each was as poor (or as rich) as the other. The girl, whose name was Mandy, was well matched with the Duke and she rather enjoyed her role as "The Duchess." They had a large and happy family.

In the movies with cowboys Tim mingled

On his wellingtons silver spurs jingled

Hopalong made him quiver

Jesse James made him shiver

And with Billy the Kid he just tingled

2

A MASS FOR BILLY THE KID

The "Grand" Cinema in Roggart specialized in Western or Cowboy films which delighted Timmy Deery and most of the male patrons. The ladies preferred romantic stories but these were always in short supply. The male owners ensured that this was the case. One Saturday the main feature was a western called "Billy the Kid." The kid, dressed all in black with silver trimmings and riding on a white horse, was portrayed as a kind of cowboy Robin Hood figure and was a particular favourite of Timmy's. At the end of the film, however, the hero, Billy, was shot dead by sheriff Pat Garrett.

Timmy Deery was greatly upset at the killing of this much-loved cowboy. He complained to everyone that he met on his way home about how unfair it was and he stayed awake that night wondering how he could get revenge on Sheriff Garrett. He went to Mass on the following day, which was Sunday, and when he heard the priest announce that the Mass was for some special people in the parish who had died, he had an idea which made him smile. He would honour the Kid with a special Mass right here in Roggart. When the service was over he went into the church vestry to request the priest to say the Mass for William Bonney (the Kid's real name). He could hear a woman's voice talking loudly as he entered. Father Muldoon was folding his vestments carefully and placing them in a shallow wooden drawer, while he chatted, but mainly listened, to Mrs O'Gorman, an elderly, loquacious, self-opinionated lady, who was discussing the flower decoration of the alter for next week. She talked about the colours she was going to use, where she got the flowers—some she got in the local florists, some she grew in her own garden, others from her neighbour's garden. The (largely one-sided) conversation went on and on. Timmy moved restlessly from one foot to the other.

'Come on, woman; finish your blooming flowers,' he muttered under his breath.

Father Muldoon looked bored but nodded politely every now and then. Mrs O'Gorman continued relentlessly.

'I would love to use orchids but they are so expensive and most people here are too ignorant (she rolled her eyes towards where Timmy was fidgeting) to appreciate them. No, I'll use some gladioli and maybe a few snap-dragons.'

'You're a right snap-dragon,' Timmy thought to himself.

At long last she finished, although she was still going on about the flowers as she went out the door and down the steps. Father Muldoon turned to Timmy.

'And what can we do for you, Timmy?' he said wearily.

'I want you to say a mass for someone that died, Father.'

'Well, I'll be delighted to do that for you, what's the name of this person?'

'William Bonney, father.'

'Bonney, Bonney, I don't know that name. Is he from Ballygore parish?'

'Ah no, father, he died over the ocean, in America.'

'Was he buried over there?'

'Eh, yes, he was, father, definitely he was.'

'So, Bill Bonney lies over the ocean,' said Father Muldoon dryly.

But his joke was lost on Timmy. They could smell the dinner being prepared in the adjacent parochial house and Father Muldoon, who had not eaten for several hours, was relieved when his housekeeper, Miss Grindly, stuck her head round the door and shouted, 'Come on to your dinner, Father, the tay is wet.'

Father Muldoon rapidly cut the conversation with Timmy short.

'Leave that to me, Timmy, I'll say the Mass for the late Mr Bonney next Sunday.'

Timmy thanked the priest profusely as he was ushered out the door. The next Sunday he sat in the front seat in the church and was delighted when "the Kid's" name was read out. We all wondered who Bonney was and if he was related to someone locally. Some people said he was from Scotland and had gone there in the 1920's to pick potatoes. Others surmised that it might be a relation of the Bonney Brothers who were a family of travelling show people that came around every few years and put on variety shows in the local parish hall. Nobody thought of asking Timmy and at the end of the day nobody was any the wiser.

Timmy made a note in his diary (an old school copybook). "This time next year a second anniversary mass to be arranged for Billy the Kid."

Timmy's friends were all highly elated

For the great wedding feast they all waited

But his plans went off beam

When he woke from his dream

And the guests to carouse were frustrated

3

THE WEDDING BREAKFAST

Timmy Deery's favourite film star was Mary Beth Miller, a co-star or bit player to the better known leading ladies. She always ended up broken-hearted and Timmy felt sorry for her. He day-dreamed sometimes about taking her out to a quiet saloon or, maybe, to a restaurant. He did not frequent the local bars, because he disliked the taste of beer, but one night he went into The Cozy Bar to buy cigarettes and Sonny was there with Mick and Jimmy McGrath, two neighbouring brothers. They had sold cattle that day in the market and were in a jovial mood.

They pressed Timmy to join in their celebration and would not take "no" for an answer. The result was that Timmy ended up "a bit merry" even though he only had three or four beers.

'Are you sure you'll be all right getting home, Timmy?' said Sonny, as Timmy lurched towards the door.

'Of course he'll be all right,' chorused the McGrath's in unison.

Timmy staggered along the road using the green bicycle as a prop. On the edge of town there was a lone telephone box and he stopped there for a rest. He felt kind of sad but happy as well. He went into the box and read an advertisement on the wall. "Book the Wonderbar Hotel for Your Ideal Wedding Breakfast. Telephone Roggart 121." Timmy's eyes lit up. He laughed aloud and rubbed his hands. He lifted the receiver and twisted the handle on the side of the box.

'Number, please?' squeaked a woman's voice. Timmy could not answer with excitement.

'What number do you require?' came the squeaky voice again.

'Roggart 121,' he spluttered.

He awoke next morning lying fully clothed on the bed. His head was splitting. He had no recollection of getting home and the noise of the children downstairs was reverberating through his head. Three days later a letter arrived in the post for him.

This was most unusual. He did not open it until he finished work that evening at eight o'clock. He read the letter over and over again. It was headed "The Wonderbar Hotel" and Timmy grew more troubled as he pored over the contents.

Dear Mr Deery,
We wish to acknowledge with thanks your valued order received by telephone today for our Premium Menu Wedding breakfast and we confirm your details as follows:—Wedding breakfast for twenty people on Saturday, 30th July, commencing at 12am.

We congratulate and compliment you on your wise choice of our hotel for your wedding breakfast and we assure you and Miss Mary Beth, as well as your guests that you will receive the most excellent meal and that you and your lovely bride will be treated like royalty.

With renewed thanks and assuring you of our best attention
Yours faithfully,
William P. G. Greetwell,
Manager.

Timmy was shocked. He would never arrange anything for a Saturday because this might interfere with his going to the cinema. Even more unpleasant scenarios flashed through his mind—he could be prosecuted, fined, maybe jailed, the shame this would bring. Something would have to be done to rectify the situation.

Eventually he heard a voice shouting from downstairs. 'Timmy are you all right? Your tay is wet and it's getting cold.'

It was Henrietta, his sister-in-law, who had been shouting at him for several minutes but Timmy had not heard her. 'I'm coming,' he shouted, and stuffing the letter into his pocket, ambled sheepishly downstairs. He ate without enthusiasm while Henrietta continued to mutter about his recent strange behaviour. Timmy thought about the letter for days. He kept to his usual routine of work on the farm and going to the cinema.

"The Great Waltz," a film biography of Johann Strauss, the great Austrian composer, was the main feature on the Saturday night and as he watched the Viennese nobility twirling around to the strains of "The Beautiful Blue Danube" a plan began to form in his head.

He even laughed aloud and people in front looked around quizzically to see who was laughing at a serious point in the film. The usherette shone her torch in the direction of the laugh. Timmy had closed his eyes and crouched down as low as possible in his seat.

When he got home that night he took a writing pad from Henrietta's kitchen dresser and sat down in his room to write an answer to the hotel. (His expertise in handwriting came from years of writing in school copy-books what he considered important facts from the films he had seen—such as "The name of Ken Maynard's horse is Tarzan" or "Tyrone Power was the best ever Jesse James.") His imagination raced along, inspired by that evening's film.

He wrote

Dear Sir,
The wedding breakfast booked for next Saturday week in your hotel will have to be cancelled due to unforeseen circumstances. The bride had to go unexpectedly to Vienna on this morning's train. Her first husband, who had gone there to a waltzing competition, has turned up having been missing for a year believed drowned in the Danube.
However, the twenty breakfasts ordered will be eaten by me on Saturday mornings over the coming weeks, so there will be no loss to your excellent hotel.
Yours faithfully,
Timothy Deery

'Damn clever, Timmy boy, a master-stroke,' he thought, as he sealed the letter.

He would drop it into the hotel on his next visit to town.

That was when I first met Timmy, a red-faced, pleasant man, about the same age as my father. I was in the hotel reception, where I worked, and he handed in a letter.

'This is important, lad,' he said, 'Make sure the manager gets it immediately.'

I assured him I would give it to the manager myself.

'Timmy Deery thanks you kindly lad,' he said.

I immediately brought the letter to the manager's office. The manager took it and bade me to stay for a moment as he opened it.

'What a strange communication!' he uttered as he scanned the contents of Timmy's letter. And handing it to me he said, 'what do you make of that?'

I read it over and shook my head. 'The man seems to have a problem. It seems to me that we'll have him for breakfast for the next twenty Saturday mornings.'

And we did.

A schoolboy who fell from a horse

His mind took a turn for the worse

His mother felt weak

When she heard the horse speak

'Cause it had a Meath accent, of course.

4

THE BLACK PONY

I had often heard my father speak of Timmy Deery and that evening I asked him about their school days together. He told me that Timmy was a good scholar and that they played together on the school football team. Timmy was also a good singer and a leading member of the school choir. At lunchtime the boys would gaze at a black pony which grazed peaceably in the paddock behind the school. They christened it "Blackie" and twelve year old Timmy would reach through the fence and rub its nose. One day Timmy persuaded two boys (one of whom was my father) to give him a lift up on Blackie's back. The pony stood quietly for a few moments and such was Timmy's elation that he began to whoop like a cowboy and the frightened animal quickly threw him on the hard ground and galloped off across the paddock. On hearing the commotion other pupils rushed over and the headmaster, who had been looking out of his window, raced outside and, with a face as black as thunder, ordered my father and the other boy to go immediately to his office. Then he and another teacher carried the still stunned and unconscious Timmy into the school.

Timmy woke up lying on a wooden bench inside the classroom. The boys who had assisted him were standing in a corner, their faces creased in pain. They were deeply upset at what happened to Timmy and also because of the pain they felt from the headmaster's cane which now lay on his desk.

'How do you feel now, Timothy Deery?' said the headmaster.

'Sore head, sir.'

'You're lucky that's all that's sore. I'm surprised at an intelligent boy like you.'

Timmy's older brother, Sonny, was ordered to take him home. They say that his mother, Margaret, was so worried about him that she wanted him brought to hospital. However, he recovered sufficiently to come to school the next day and appeared none the worse for his escapade. The headmaster had the pony moved away from the school. About a month or so after these events things started to go less well at school for Timmy. He lost his place on the school football team and from being one of the top pupils academically he began to slip down into the bottom half of his class. From then until the end of primary school Timmy continued to regress and somehow got left behind the other pupils. The only activity in which he did not slip back was the choir. He loved to sing and to this day he is still one of the finest singers you could wish to hear.

When it came to moving on from primary school there were many stories about why Timmy never made it to secondary. It is said that Margaret Deery, Timmy's mother, blamed the headmaster. Certainly there was a difficult meeting between Timmy's parents and the headmaster and that his mother fought vainly that he should go to secondary school. She said fourteen was too young an age to start work. The headmaster, apparently, advised her that Timmy's examination results were so poor that he would not be able for it. His father said he could do with more help on the farm and that was the deciding factor. Margaret Deery always maintained that until the pony incident he was the most intelligent of her seven children, four of whom became doctors.

Margaret Deery's life also changed at this time. She was no longer the jolly open-hearted person with the infectious laugh so beloved of her family and friends. Sometimes her thoughts were as black as the pony whose wild outline and flashing eyes were ever in her mind. About one year after Timmy left school, on a cool evening in late autumn, Margaret had another unusual experience, which, again, changed her life, but this time for the better. She became more serene and contented with life.

The rest of the family had been gone from early morning to Roggart, as it was market day and they had cattle to sell. An exhausted Margaret had flopped down in the wooden armchair in front of the open range. The dark kitchen was lit only by the bright and flickering logs as she was too tired to light the oil lamp after a crowded day of cleaning, bedding, milking and feeding on the busy farm. Her eyelids felt heavy as she half dozed and followed the fluttering fireplace shadows through half closed eyes. There was a noise outside and then a muffled knock on the door.

'Come in,' she said, and then in a more raised voice, 'it's not locked.'

The door swung open and framed in the doorway was none other than the black pony. Margaret eyed him suspiciously. He seemed smaller and more docile and quite unlike the wild red-eyed creature which had haunted her thoughts since the time of Timmy's accident.

'What brings you here? Is it to gloat over what you did to my son?'

She spoke calmly and, strangely enough, she felt quite calm and was unsurprised when the pony answered her in a deep but clear male type voice.

'I come on a mission. Humans talk about "horse sense" but they seldom show any. My advice for you is this. Remove the blinkers which you have worn for the past year and you will see a fuller picture of your son. Timothy is content in his own wonderful world. His gifts are many:- a tranquil mind; nature's fields, rivers, lakes and hills; the music of his voice; his imaginary world of cinema; friendships; family love; coming together in church; his uncomplicated honesty and frankness. You must not make a halter to lead him like an ass. You are a wise woman and I wish you well.'

Before she could answer, the black pony whirled around and, as he went through the doorway, his rear hooves kicked back and clipped the door shut. Margaret Deery listened until the galloping sound faded away, then her eyes closed and she drifted into a deep sleep. She awoke to find her husband and other family members chattering and laughing about all they had seen at the market. She hugged a startled Timmy who was reading a Tom Mix comic which his father had bought for him. He responded 'Ah, mam, that mushy stuff is barred in the Wild West.'

They all laughed. Mr Deery asked how her day had been and had she done anything exciting.

'Oh, nothing too exciting,' she replied, 'just horsing around as usual.'

The following day at breakfast Timmy said 'I wonder what knocked a lump of paint out of the kitchen door.'

Oilly planned his fair wife to beguile

With his head soaked in paraffin oil

But the smell from his pate

So frustrated his mate

That it caused her to go off the boil

5

WAR AND PEACE

Timmy Deery was a simple man. Yet, there came a time when all of Timmy's neighbours agreed that, on this occasion, he had shown the wisdom of Solomon. It all centred on a seemingly intractable dispute between two elderly brothers who lived in the neighbourhood.

Andy and Oilly Malooney were two brothers who married two sisters and lived in two adjoining houses in the Meath countryside near the small town of Roggart. They were now old and retired from work. When they were young men they were very close and shared everything. They worked hard together on the farm. They got married in the same church on the same day.

They built their two houses adjoining one another and put an interconnecting door in the common adjoining wall so that they and their families could move freely between each other's homes. In fact it was like one big house with one big family living in it. Well, maybe not a "big" big house, because in those days people only built houses big enough to eat and sleep in, with a kitchen and one or two bedrooms. If visitors called (and visitors were always calling in those days) they were entertained in the kitchen and they, of course, also entertained the people of the house, by bringing news and stories from around the countryside.

In appearance the two brothers looked completely different. Oilly still had a thick head of (now grey) hair while Andy had become totally bald. Oilly was very proud of what he called his "well thatched roof" and he always judged other men by how much hair they had. This irritated Andy.

'Oh, your man is going bald,' Oilly would say derisively. 'He must be on the way out.'

When he was twelve years old he had heard an old neighbour, who was a respected animal quack, say that paraffin oil, which was used as fuel for lanterns, was a powerful agent for growing human hair. And so he kept a bottle of this under his bed and every night he rubbed a liberal amount into his prized tresses. This was why he was called "Oilly." His real name was 'Oliver.' He was ten years married when his wife gave him an ultimatum. The poor woman had endured, with great fortitude, the stinking paraffin fumes and the grimy pillow cases, not to mention the danger of the kids lighting matches. He had recently begun to mix a very pungent tractor TVO oil to the paraffin.

'Either that oily concoction goes or I go!' she said, seething with rage.

She'd been gone about six weeks when, by a strange coincidence, Andy's wife also upped stakes and left. This occurred because she objected to having to cook and wash for both families.

When the two brothers became too old to work on the farm their sons took it over and it was around this time that the trouble between them started. Both Andy and Oilly had shown little interest in politics (or indeed in anything other than farming) until after they retired. They would usually chase away whatever politicians called to their door at election time (on one occasion Andy ushered a politician off the premises at the point of a four-grained dung fork) but this time things were different. A local election took place in the county and Andy and Oilly had a major falling out over which candidate they would vote for. The candidate who lived nearest to them was Sylvie Dianne—an active loquacious man of sixty years old and Andy decided that he was the man for the job but Oilly had one big reservation about Sylvie. The poor man was as bald as an egg and Oilly maintained that Joe Jameson, who was a Ronald Reagan look-a-like, with the finest head of black hair you ever saw, was the superior candidate. Anyway Joe Jameson won the seat by a narrow margin and that night Oilly joined in the celebrations. One of the brother's fields high up on a hill was known as the "Furzy Field" because it was covered by a large number of furze bushes. A tradition in the neighbourhood was to light bonfires outside at night to mark all kinds of successes, such as football victories, weddings, and elections.

Andy was in a foul mood that evening. Not only had he backed the wrong man in the election, but he had spent the past two hours lighting the kitchen range and preparing a cabbage and bacon dinner for himself and Oilly. He had even wet the tay and now there was no sign of his brother, also it had got quite dark outside. And then Andy got a shock. Looking out the back window he noticed a fire up on the hill behind the house. Then suddenly more fires started to appear and soon there were about twenty of them with flames leaping up into the dark night sky.

'Gad damn it, the furzy field is being burned,' he shouted to himself.

Then grabbing an old shotgun which they used for frightening crows in the potato field Andy raced out of the house and up the hill to the furzy field. There were figures flitting about whooping and laughing in the semi darkness. Andy began firing the shotgun, at first up in the air and then seeing no reaction he fired a blast lower down. He heard someone scream and the shouting died down. He then found himself surrounded by a dumbfounded crowd of men, most of whom he knew as his friends and neighbours from the locality.

'What the hell is going on here?' Andy shouted.

'We were just burning a few furze for Joe Jameson's great win in the election,' said Sonny Deery, who was Andy's next door neighbour. 'What the hell do you think you're doing with that oul gun?'

'You're only after shooting your own brother,' said Timmy Deery.

'You're a goddam infernal idiot,' said Ivor Nale.

Andy was shocked to the core. 'He, he's not dead is he? Ooh good God almighty, I deserve to be hung for this.'

Oilly moaned and held his arm. He had received a slight graze on his upper arm.

'Are, are you all right, are you all right, speak to us, are you bleeding?'

Andy had got a far greater scare than his brother. In fact, he was in a state of shock.

Sonny gently took the old gun from him and checked it to make sure the cartridge cylinder was empty. Then putting it across his shoulder he walked away, leaving Andy and Oilly to settle their differences between themselves.

A shower of rain started to fall but it did nothing to diminish Oilly's temper. He was fuming with rage. He shouted at everyone within earshot to quench all the fires, most of which had already gone out because of the rain. Andy was still in shock after realizing that he could have killed his own brother. He stood open-mouthed and trembling. Oilly stalked off without a word and headed straight home to his house.

Andy stood alone among the black ash residue of the recently burnt furze bushes. After about ten minutes he began shuffling slowly towards the house with a heavy heart. He thought there was only one bright spot among the travails of the evening and that was the fact that Oilly seemed to have received no serious injury at all. True, he was in a rage because he had been shot at by his own brother, and in front of all his neighbours. This hurt his pride and put him in a bad temper. The trouble with this was that, while Andy was quick-tempered, he was also quick to forgive and forget, while Oilly was the direct opposite. Oilly would hold this grudge forever and a day against his brother. Andy eventually reached home and seeing the light in Oilly's house he thought he had better apologize for what happened. He twisted the doorknob as usual but found the door was locked. He knocked a few times but got no response so he went into his own house and went to the interconnecting door between the two houses. Here he got a shock. The door was gone and the space was filled up crudely with six-inch solid concrete blocks. There were piles of wet cement splashed on his floor after the hastily botched block building. Oilly certainly meant business.

The next morning Andy awoke to the sound of hammering and banging from behind the blocked-up doorway. Somebody was knocking down the blocks, some of which fell into Andy's side and on to his parlour or sitting room floor. A loud whistling was heard and Andy recognized Ivor Nale. He shouted through at Ivor.

'What the hell is going on out there, Ivor is that you? What on earth are you doing?

'I'm rebuilding these blocks for Oilly. He was banging on my door at six o'clock this morning, said it had to be done immediately. He said he's not setting foot in this house until your place is completely closed off, sorry Andy but I'm just following orders.'

Andy was dumbstruck. Ivor started a shrill rendition of "The Whistling Gypsy" as he went about his work. Ivor was a skilled block-layer and it only took him half an hour or so to rebuild the crude wall which Oilly had thrown up the previous evening. He plastered Oilly's side of the wall and whistled away as he stepped back and admired his handiwork. Then he went outside and around to Andy's house, whistling as usual. The door was open so he went straight in.

'I was wondering if you want your side plastered up, Andy?, it'd finish it off nice and neat.'

'Oh do whatever you like, Ivor, my life is finished here,' said Andy mournfully.

'Ah, things are never as bad as they seem, they always get sorted out in the end. You'll see Andy, auld pal, keep your chin up.'

That evening Ivor had another job to do fixing up an old wall for the Deery's. As he worked and Sonny and Timmy assisted by carrying blocks they talked about the worsening situation in the feud between the two elderly brothers.

Sonny said, 'The best way to bring those two together is to throw a bucket of water over them or even a bag of flour.'

Timmy said nothing, but Sonny's observation about the bag of flour stuck in his mind. That night he had a brainwave. He had always seen Andy and Oilly going to the village church every Saturday afternoon to confessions. They had done this for about sixty years and generally walked in together. Timmy was used to getting bags of flour from Rattlestown Mill for Henrietta to bake bread. So on Saturday after his lunch he put the white cloth flour bag in the basket of his green bike and headed for the mill. He got two stone weight of the whitest flour and hid himself behind a bush near the church door. But things did not work out as he expected. Oilly arrived on his own and he still

27

looked angry. As he passed the bush and went into the church Timmy observed Andy trudging along to the church about two hundred yards behind his brother. Andy then went inside and Timmy followed him still carrying the bag of flour. As Andy reached the seat beside the confession box who comes out of the box right beside him only Oilly. The two of them froze and Timmy seized his chance. He upturned the bag of flour over the two men. Some of the flour fell into the confession box on top of Father Muldoon and he leaped out to see what was going on. Mrs O'Gorman who was arranging flowers on the altar, screamed and then when she saw who was involved rushed forward and started berating Timmy.

'I saw this lout spilling flour over these poor men and all over the church, he's ruined the whole place,' she shrieked.

The two brothers looked like two white ghosts with flour covering them from head to toe. Fr Muldoon said nothing for a few seconds, as he quickly sized up the situation. Then he started roaring with laughter. On seeing the priest laugh Oilly began to laugh and Andy then began to laugh. Then Timmy himself joined in the laughter. Mrs O'Gorman still looked like thunder. 'Is everyone here gone stark raving mad?' she yelped.

The priest put his arms around the two brothers. 'Come with me, lads, and you too, Timmy, this calls for a celebratory drink, now only a little one mind. We'll leave Mrs O'Gorman in peace. No use crying over spilt flour, Haw, haw, haw.'

Ivor Nale got another job that day, knocking down the blocked up doorway and refitting the original wooden door for the, now reconciled, Andy and Oilly.

Ivor's belle, lovely Rosie, was worried

His forty year courtship unhurried

She feared that herself

Would be left on the shelf

And as an old maid she'd be buried

6

IN THE BACK ROW

Buddy Bryson was known as the "J. Arthur Rank" of Roggart. He had started his cinema in the 1940's in an old galvanized tin shed which his father owned just off Main Street. The shed, which was used during the day to store a hay slide, a corn winnowing machine, and some horse harness, was christened "The Grand." For each performance the hay slide had to be removed from the shed and replaced by seating and Buddy always had willing helpers to do this as there would be free admission for his "assistants." One of his assistants was Timmy Deery, who delightedly did any heavy work, such as moving equipment in and out and arranging the seating. The seating mostly consisted of wooden planks placed on old cement blocks with about a dozen old tubular chairs. Jem Bryce took the money at the door and Buddy himself worked the projector from the top of the winnowing machine which provided a solid foundation. Frequently the film would break down, if the reels had not been rewound properly by the previous user. The early films were always made in black and white and when the first colour film arrived the excitement was unbelievable. This was "The Great Caruso" with Mario Lanza and Ann Blyth. The film ran for three weeks and many went to see it several times. Everyone in town was singing operatic arias for months afterwards.

Timmy Deery was fifteen years old when he first visited Roggart on his own. He had heard about the new "Grand" picture house from Ivor Nale and the first film he saw was a horror piece called "Invasion of the Worms." His favourite western was "Canadian Pacific" starring Randolph Scott. It was the story of the building of the railway across Canada and Timmy was so smitten that he was hooked on western films from that time onwards. He was given a special seat in the middle back row with his back leaning against the winnowing machine and nobody dared take that seat, or there would be the mother and father of a row. Many young couples who were going out together frequented the "Grand" and, much to Timmy's annoyance, they always crowded into the back row and he seemed to be squashed in the middle of them. Also, they did not always pay much attention to the action on the screen, but kissed and cuddled, ate sweets and talked in whispers.

One evening Timmy was standing outside waiting for the programme to start, and Ivor Nale, who was in his late fifties, and many years older than Timmy, came along with a lady called Rosie, whom Timmy knew as Ivor's girl friend. They had been going out together for the best part of forty years and the ladies of the village sewing circle had long since given up on seeing them walk down the aisle.

'Poor Rosie,' they would say, 'imagine being strung along by that lug of a Nale fellow, sure he'll never propose to her, wasted the best years of her life waiting on that miserable wretch.'

Sonny, one day, commented that Rosie herself had recently said to Ivor, 'I think we should get married,' and Ivor replied, 'Sure who in their right mind would have either of us.' Sonny thought this was a great joke and roared laughing. Timmy did not understand what he was laughing at.

Anyway, on this occasion, there was a third person accompanying the older couple. It was Rosie's niece, a pleasant looking girl of about seventeen and she smiled at Timmy, who blushed and looked upwards at the night sky, pretending he was interested in the stars.

'That's Jupiter up there,' he said to Ivor.

'Really,' said the girl, in a posh English sounding accent, 'I thought Jupiter was only visible from the southern hemisphere.'

Timmy glared at Ivor who seemed intent on prolonging the conversation. Putting one arm around the girl's shoulders and the other around Timmy's he pushed the two of them so close together that Timmy's nose touched the girl's forehead.

'Timmy, this is Wendy, here on holiday from England, Wendy this is Timmy,' he said cheerily, 'Now you two go in there together and discuss the stars. This is my treat. Here, Timmy, here's a bag of sweets.'

There was no use arguing with Ivor. Rosie murmured for him to leave them alone and that maybe they did not want to discuss the planets. But Wendy was glad to have someone nearer to her own age to talk to. She had been staying with her Aunt Rosie for a week now and was a bit bored.

She followed Timmy in and sat down beside him. The first film was a Roy Rogers cowboy, which did not really interest her. However, as soon as it began, Timmy became totally immersed in it. He forgot completely about the young English girl sitting beside him. He opened the bag of sweets which Ivor had given him and began eating them and at the same time being transfixed by the action on screen. Wendy waited patiently to be offered one, but in a few minutes Timmy had emptied the whole bag of marshmallows. He burped as the last one went down. One of Timmy's jobs at the cinema was to switch on the lights for the interval but on this night he forgot to switch them on. As the first film ended Buddy waited for a few seconds and when nothing happened he leaned down from the top of the winnowing machine to see where Timmy was and the reel of film which he was holding in his hand caught on a protruding part of the machine and flew forward in an arc and landed on the tray of ice-cream which the usherette held in readiness to sell to the patrons.

Needless to say, the reel fell out of its box, as Buddy had opened the catch. There was much cursing and swearing by Buddy and his friends as they attempted to rewind the reel of film. The crowd was good-humoured and was used to diversionary interruptions although this one was a more exciting sideshow than usual. Eventually the show got going again but several times the screen filled with strange flashing shapes and the story was out of sequence.

Timmy got a tongue-lashing from Buddy and was in a huff at the end of the show. Sonny had arranged to give Ivor a lift home and so himself, Rosie, Wendy and Timmy all piled into Sonny's old Hillman Minx for the lift. Rosie lived at the end of a mile-long narrow lane, which was in bad repair. It was a fine summer's night and, as he pulled up at the entrance to Rosie's lane Sonny said, 'It's a lovely night for a walk in the moonlight, the old car would get lost in those potholes, so it would.'

'Yeah,' said Rosie, 'The road-men are always going to fix them.'

Sonny switched off the engine and as nobody moved he began whistling to himself.

'Well, lads,' he said, looking 'round at Ivor and Timmy.

'Well, what?' said Ivor.

'Are yez going to escort these girls down the lane?'

'Well, now, a fellow would have to think about that.'

At this remark Rosie brusquely opened the door and got out.

'Come on Wendy, good night, Sonny, and thanks for the lift.'

As the two girls set off, Ivor wound down the side window and called after them, 'goodnight to yez,' while Timmy muttered 'g'night.'

Sonny turned to Ivor and Timmy.

'Yez are a grand pair, letting those poor girls find their own way down that dark lane at night.'

'Well, Rosie is long enough walking that lane to know her own way by now,' said Ivor as he settled into his seat. 'Anyway, they have a flash lamp.'

Oilly's hair they cut off at the root,

But he got a new hat which looked cute

This made the girls dizzy

And all in a tizzy.

The scoffers it caused to be mute.

7

HEAD OR HARP?

Andy and Oilly Malooney had become friends again. Oilly, however, still held bald men in low esteem.

'There's just something lacking in them,' he confided to Timmy one day as they wound hay ropes to tie down the four large pikes of hay which stood in the corner of the Deery's haggard. The hay ropes were manoeuvred across the tops of the hay pikes by Timmy climbing up the ladder and lifting the ropes with his pitchfork. He was on the last rope when his fork caught in a piece of wire which was attached to a high branch of a large tree.

'Drat,' said Timmy, as the wire fell to the ground. 'That's the radio banjaxed.'

The aerial for the Deery's radio consisted of about fifty yards of woven copper wire attached to a socket on the back of the radio. This was fed out through the back parlour window and attached to a high branch on an old elm tree.

'We'll have to leave it for now or I'll be late for the pictures, I'll fix it tomorrow.'

Timmy jumped up on his green bicycle and pedalled off furiously, leaving Oilly to tidy up the haggard.

'Ah, the young people nowadays, always rushing for everything. Bedad in my day things were different.' Oilly's mutterings were suddenly interrupted by a woman's voice and an angry woman's voice at that.

'Did you dimwits knock down the radio aerial?' demanded Mrs Deery. 'Well you better get it up again and quickly because Din-Joe is on in ten minutes time and that's one program that I'm not going to miss.'

'Oh, bedad, mam, you could never afford to miss Din-Joe. He plays only lovely music so he does. He had a fella playin' the fiddle last—'

'You'll be playing the harp if that aerial is not fixed now, at once, immediately,' Mrs Deery interrupted.

'Don't worry, Mam, I won't be a minute putting it up again,' said Oilly.

Oilly picked up the end of the wire and looked up at the tree. There was a lowish branch which he decided would do to hook the wire on to and as luck would have it a tar barrel stood underneath the branch. Oilly clambered onto the barrel and managed to attach the aerial to the tree.

'Now, Mrs Deery, you can listen to all the Din-Joes you like,' he muttered to himself. 'There was none of these modern "Din-Joes" squawking out of radios in my day.'

But as he was getting down, the barrel, which contained a couple of gallons of tar, slipped from underneath him and he rolled to the ground to find himself covered in slimy thick tar. His face escaped but his clothes and hair did not. With much cursing and swearing he picked himself up and surveyed the damage. His old clothes were ruined but that did not worry him. His hair was the only part of his body to be affected. His treasured tresses were stuck solid with this horrible black tacky substance. He quickly tidied up the haggard and headed for home.

Andy met him at the gate and stared in amazement at the apparition before him.

'What on earth happened, were you tarred and feathered?' Andy said.

'No, I was only tarred, have you the tay wet?'

As they ate, Oilly related what happened. He told Andy to put on the kettle and boil some water for a bath.

'You're not due a bath until next week,' Andy grumbled, 'however, we'll try it.'

Despite much vigorous scrubbing with soap and hot water the tar remained. They used all the butter and grease they could find and rubbed it into the hair but there was little improvement.

'There's only one thing for it,' said Andy, 'the hair will have to be cut off. I'll get the scissors.'

Oilly sat meekly on a kitchen chair while Andy attempted to cut off his tar-filled locks. It was proving much more difficult than the two brothers imagined. Having got as much of the tar out as was possible with the scissors Andy stood back and stroked his chin as he gazed at the miserable vision that sat like Humpty Dumpty on the chair in front of him.

'You look like a cross between a billiard ball and a dead blackbird,' Andy observed, 'I'll tell you what, we'll have to shave the rest of it off with the old cut-throat, the hair should grow back again in time!'

Andy went to work with gusto. He was beginning to actually enjoy the episode. He scraped away with the old razor, sharpening the blade every now and then by rubbing it along the strop. After a half hour of scratching and scraping and listening to Oilly moaning, groaning and swearing, Andy held up an old mirror into which Oilly gazed disbelievingly.

'I'm ruined,' he whined, 'all me beautiful hair that I lavished such care and attention on for the past forty years, it's gone, gone, gone!'

'Hey, if you put music to that, you'd have a song!' said Andy brightly. 'I think that in six months time you will have a fine head of hair. In the meantime you'll just have more face to wash, like I have, going right back to the nape of me neck.'

Over the following couple of days Oilly felt like some kind of freak show. Word had spread that he had gone bald and in a rural backwater this news was on a par with Martians invading Earth. People went out of their way to see the phenomenon and Oilly, who had never worn a cap or a hat because he had been so proud of his fine head of hair, decided that he would have to invest in some class of headgear.

'I was just wondering,' he said to Andy, with a worried look on his face, 'How much do you think would a fairly dacent hat cost?'

Andy was always very wary when talking about money. He stroked his chin and looked extremely serious.

'Well I would hazard a guess, give or take, all things considered, the time of the year and whether you want a top of the range or an auld caibin, you could be looking at the guts of anything from five bob to twelve and sixpence,' he mused.

'On the other hand. .'

'Yes, Yes,' Oilly impatiently cut him short, 'you don't have to go on and on like a wet week, I'll go into Grady's in Roggart first thing tomorrow morning.'

Grady's was the only man's drapery shop in Roggart. It was a large ground floor premises with heavy wooden counters and from the ceiling there hung a system of ropes and pulleys by which the cash takings and customer receipts and change were sent backwards and forwards between the counters and a central raised square shaped office. The store had three departments, Men's Wear, Boy's Wear and Household Textiles. There were large rolls of cloth, mainly navy blue or grey in colour, stacked on shelves on all sides of the shop. The three Grady brothers ran the business. They all looked about seventy years of age and all wore navy blue suits and had a tape measure hanging loosely around their neck.

Oilly walked past the store several times before he ventured in. He noticed a tall well-dressed man standing just inside the door who was wearing a green tweed hat. He waited until a few customers left and then entered. The tall man stared blankly at him.

'Nice day, sir, I was wondering where is the hat department?'

The man did not reply. However, one of the Grady brothers rushed over and greeted him warmly.

'Now, sir, what can we do for you?'

'I was thinking of buying a hat, now not a real dear one, mind.'

The three Grady brothers fussed around Oilly. First they tried a hat for size.

'Size eight and a half,' one of them announced. After trying on a few hats Oilly decided that a cap might suit him better.

'What a gentleman needs nowadays is a hat for Sundays and formal occasions and a cap for workdays,' said one Grady.

'Oh yes,' said another, 'that's exactly what a gentleman requires.'

'How much would that set me back?' said Oilly.

The third Grady piped up. 'It would not set you back, it would propel you forward.'

'For you, we'll do a special deal,' said the first Grady, 'fifteen shillings for the two, you'll never get a better offer.'

As Oilly hummed and hawed about how dear things were the second Grady intervened. 'Shall we wrap the two for you, sir, or perhaps you want to wear that hat?'

'It certainly suits you,' said the third Grady.

Oilly looked down at the man who was still standing at the door. 'Bedad, I think I'll wear it. It certainly suits yer man.'

As he left the shop Oilly stopped in front of the tall man and pointed at his new hat.

'You and me, two of a kind, we have good taste in hats. Good luck to ye sir.'

'He seems very interested in that old display mannequin,' said one Grady as Oilly went out of the shop.

He looked at himself in every shop window as he passed along the street wearing the dark green hat with a small red feather on one side. His mind was still in a whirl of excitement an hour later when he reached home.

'Bedad, you got some bargain there,' said Andy, 'fifteen bob you say, I think I'll invest meself.'

'Well, I thought they charged me over the odds and that they were right tricksters. If it wasn't for that other customer I was telling you about, ah a terrible quiet poor divil, the hat looked so well on him, that's what made up my mind for me.'

Oilly wore the hat all that day and did not take it off even when he ate or when he shaved or washed. The first Sunday he visited the Deery household, as he often did, and Mrs Deery went into ecstasies of admiration when she saw Oilly's new hat. Timmy asked him about where he bought it and whether they sold ten gallon cowboy hats. Oilly laughed and said, 'Well, they were definitely right cowboys so I'm sure they must sell cowboy hats.'

'Is that right?' said Timmy, 'I must get one.'

The next day Timmy met Oilly and this time he was wearing his new cap. Timmy stared at it and commented, 'I prefer the hat, why are you wearing a cap?'

'Oh, I keep the hat for my Sunday head and this is for my weekday head.'

Timmy looked startled. 'You mean you have two heads.'

'Aye, Timmy, that's what gives me a head start over you ordinary chaps.'

Timmy innocently spread this story around and in time Oilly became known as the man with two heads.

Every weekday from that time onward Oilly wore the cap and every Sunday the hat. And, eventually, after about six months when his hair did grow back to its former glory he had become so fond of the headgear that he continued to wear it and he never again belittled bald men. His own months of "baldness" had taught him a valuable lesson.

The maid was the belle of the ball

With a frock that was not her's at all

In a weakness she took it

When Tim kicked the bucket

And she boogied all night in the Hall

8

DRESSING DOWN

Every summer a carnival week was held in Roggart to raise funds for the parish. A large marquee was erected in the football field and every night a dance was held in it. The highlight was the final Sunday night when the Carnival Queen was selected. Judges were brought in from the neighbouring parishes and there was great rivalry among the girls.

Una McKay was a very good-looking nineteen year old who worked in one of the big houses in the area. She was a kitchen maid for the Babington family and was the fourth eldest of five sisters. She was poorly paid in money terms but got all her meals in the house. The only other concession to the staff was that any old shoes or boots which the family had no further use for would be given to them. One day Una was asked by the head of kitchen staff if she was interested in a pair of red sling-back shoes which Lady Babington had thrown out. The young girl was thrilled and said, 'Oh yes, please, yes, please.'

She brought home the prized shoes wrapped in newspaper and, even though they were a size too big for her and the buckle of one was bent and twisted where something heavy had fallen on it, to Una this was a minor flaw and could easily be hammered out and repaired. Now if only she had a red dress to go with the shoes!

She looked forward eagerly to the carnival and entering the Carnival Queen competition. Her biggest problem was that the only suitable dress she had was a green one which had been handed down from her older sister. To make matters worse her sister, Jane, had been selected Carnival Queen the previous year while wearing this dress. One day while having her dinner in Babington's she was leafing through a magazine belonging to Lady Babington when she came across an article on how to change the look of a frock by "tie-dyeing" it. It all sounded very easy. You simply tied the garment in knots, soaked it in a bucket of colour dye and when it was removed and untied a beautiful new coloured pattern appeared on it. Well, in the magazine, it seemed beautiful and so easy, and Una remembered that there was some red dye at home which her mother had bought but never used.

Una wasted no time. When she got home that evening she got to work. In the kitchen she prepared the bucket of red dye, tied several knots on the green frock, and pushed it into the bucket with a wooden ladle. Her mother and sisters had gone into town so she had no interruptions or objections to what she was doing.

'I must hide it until it is finished,' she thought to herself. 'Now where would be a good place? I know; the summer house.'

The summer house was a bockety wooden structure well hidden by branches of plum and apple trees and located in the McKay's overgrown garden.

'It will be safe there until tomorrow. It should be soaked enough by then,' Una mused as she carried out the bucket of bright red liquid. The next morning Una went off to work at seven o'clock as usual. She took a quick look in the summer house to make sure that the dye colouring operation had not been disturbed. Having satisfied herself that all was well she proceeded to Babington's.

Later on that morning Timmy Deery was driving five bullocks along the road past McKay's garden and one of the animals broke through the flimsy hedge which bordered the summer house. Timmy jumped off his green bicycle and shouted at the animal.

'Come back, you awkward contrary brute!' he roared, as he followed the beast.

The animal gave a buck lep and came out again on to the road without mishap but Timmy was not so lucky. He stepped right into the bucket of red dye which Una had hidden.

'What in the name of all the bad luck miserable wretches, who left that? Be the holy saints it's a bucket of blood!'

Timmy stared down at his wellington boot which was once black but now mostly red in colour. Then he remembered the cattle he was supposed to be driving. He kicked the bucket out of his way in temper and jumping on his bike, raced after them. By the time he rounded up the five bullocks and put them safely into the "top field" he had forgotten about the bucket of "blood." On reaching home, he was quickly reminded of it by Henrietta when he marched straight onto the kitchen floor which she had just washed and polished.

'Timmy Deery,' she yelled, 'What is that red stuff on my good floor? Is that blood on your foot? What on earth happened to you?'

'Oh yeah, the blood, I accidentally stepped into a bucket of blood this morning when I was driving the cattle to the top field. It was in McKay's garden.'

Timmy explained to Henrietta about one of the cattle breaking into the garden and what happened with the bucket.

'That's terrible, where could all that blood have come from?' said Henrietta.

'I dunno, maybe they killed a pig or something.'

'They don't have any livestock. I'll have to get Sonny to check on things over there. In the meantime get all that blood cleaned off your boots and then you can clean up the mess you made on my kitchen floor.'

Sonny returned at mid-day for his dinner and listened intently while Timmy and Henrietta related the events of the morning.

'Strange,' he murmured. 'Are you sure it was blood?'

'Sure what else could it be? It was red and there was a bucket of it.'

'I have me doubts, but I'll go over and have a word with the McKay's. They're quiet hard-working people. There is probably a simple explanation for all this.'

After he had eaten Sonny made his way to the McKay household. Mrs McKay was in her kitchen clearing up the dinner dishes and she greeted him warmly as she usually did.

'The tay is still wet, sure you'll have a cup.'

'Aye, sure I might as well.'

47

She was always in good humour and today was no different. After they had exchanged pleasantries and discussed the weather and Mrs McKay enquired after Henrietta she then asked how Timmy was and this gave Sonny the opening he was looking for.

'Well, it's funny you should ask about Timmy because a peculiar thing occurred this morning. He was driving the cattle to the top field and one wild one happened to break into your garden. I hope he didn't do any damage to your fruit trees.'

'Ah, not at all, sure the garden is wild. I'll get that fence fixed right away.'

'Mrs McKay, you didn't have a bucket of red liquid like fruit juice in the garden?'

'No, why?'

'Well, Timmy came home with his boots covered in red liquid and he said it happened in your garden. Do you mind if I have a look around the garden? It's probably nothing at all.'

'Oh, go right ahead, Sonny, let me know if you find anything.'

Sonny was not long in finding the bucket of red dye which Timmy had stepped in. The green dress which Una was tie-dyeing looked a sorry sight. Timmy had squashed it with his size eleven boots and most of the dye had ended up on the ground. 'That's definitely red dye for colouring clothes,' Sonny said to himself, 'probably one of the McKay geshehs and Timmy has made a right mess of it. I'll let Mrs McKay know that it's not blood anyway.'

Sonny told Mrs McKay about the dye and said he would send Timmy over to apologise and also to fix the fence which the bullock had broken through. 'That's the last we'll hear of that episode,' he said to himself as he headed for home. But it was not quite the end.

Three months later a headline appeared in the local newspaper, The Roggart News, "Servant Girl Wore Her Employer's Frock to Dance." Sonny carefully read over the case. The young girl, Una McKay, said she was desperate to go to the Carnival Queen dance. Her own dress had been ruined by a man with cattle trampling on it. She had given in to temptation. The dress fitted her perfectly. She had laundered and ironed it afterwards and returned it to its wardrobe but she had been caught in the act by Lady Babington and this had resulted in her appearance in court. She also lost her job. District Justice Raymer took a lenient view of the incident and Una McKay was let off with a warning as to her future conduct. There was laughter in court when the judge said he could not understand why some ladies held on to clothes that they wore as teenagers. Did they hope that one day scientists would discover a magic potion to reduce the middle-age spread? Perhaps Lady Babington might consider donating her old clothes to charity!

On his bench sat the judge looking fat

His white wig changed its hue as he sat

Like King Midas of old

Turned a bright shade of gold

There'll be wigs on the green, fancy that.

9

A JUDGE OF COLOUR

The District Justice for this area of Meath was Mr Edward Raymer. He lived in a rather unkempt large house reached by a long avenue. The old two story house had yellow-washed walls and wooden fencing. The locals tended to keep clear of him. For a few this was because they had appeared before his court on some minor charge, but for most it was because they wrongly assumed that a judge was someone whose revered station was beyond the ambit of ordinary people. He loved horses and followed the Ward Union Stag-hounds during the hunting season. He had never married and the most obvious signs of this were un-ironed shirts and untidy court robes. He also had the habit of over-powdering his wig as he felt that this covered up any imperfections. The court sat in Roggart on one day per month.

The Deery family frequently had visits from relations or neighbours in the evening time. The children would be sent to their room and told to do their school homework, or if school was out, they would be told to read or at least to keep quiet. Their reward the next morning would be any goodies left over from the meal which Mrs Deery provided. She always made sure that something sweet was left over, usually a bit of jelly and custard. The children were especially fond of this when it was cold and set overnight.

One evening the Deerys had a surprise visitor. A large dark green car chugged into the yard and pulled up beside the water pump. Steam was gushing out from under the bonnet. The lone occupant switched off the engine and staggered out and away from the steaming car. It was the District Justice, himself. The family were all at home and rallied to his aid.

'Don't go near it until it cools down,' Sonny shouted.

'Come in and rest, Mr Raymer, while you're waiting, the tay is wet,' said Henrietta.

51

The judge had got a bit of a shock and was glad to get out of the scalding vehicle.

'Ow thank you sow mach,' he said in his loud posh accent, 'I thought the old jalopy was gowing tow explode.'

'It'll take a half hour or so to cool down and then maybe we'll see what caused the problem,' said Sonny. 'You have a cardboard box on the back seat, I think we'll take it out in case it gets water damage.'

Sonny took out the box, which was very light, and told the children to bring it into the house for safe-keeping.

'Ow good gells,' said the judge, 'it's ownly the jolly old wig which I wear in court, pwobably requires powdering.'

Eventually the engine cooled and when Timmy started refilling it, they all saw where the problem was. The water went in at the top and straight out again at the bottom. In those days there was a safety valve which blew out if the water pressure got too high. This usually happened if the radiator was not topped up regularly. There happened to be a spare valve in Deery's shed and this fitted the judge's car. The relieved man departed with much loud thanks-giving and shaking of hands. It was about an hour later that Henrietta noticed the cardboard box sitting behind the armchair in the parlour. Sonny and Timmy were both gone to the pictures in Roggart. The children wanted to open it just to have a close-up peek at a real judge's wig.

'Well, just a quick look and don't handle it at all.'

The box was not sealed so Henrietta gently lifted the lid.

'Yuk, is it alive?' The children twisted their faces and made squealing noises.

'It's horrible, if Towser sees it he'll think it's a rabbit and eat it.'

'That's enough now,' said Henrietta as she closed the box. 'I'd better telephone Judge Raymer and tell him.'

The judge told her not to worry and he would collect the box the following morning on his way to court. Henrietta put on her coat and scarf.

'That's grand, now I have to go over to Mullards for a game of cards so, hopefully, there'll be no more emergencies for an hour or two.'

She was gone about fifteen minutes when the telephone rang. Rose, the oldest girl, went to the hall and took the call. She came back a minute later looking flustered.

'That was Mr Raymer and do you know what he wants me to do?'

'Wants you to do,' the other two replied.

'Yes, me, myself. He asked if I could dust off his wig and shake some white powder on it so that it would be ready for wearing in court tomorrow. He said there's a small squeeze container of powder in the box.'

Rose gingerly opened the box and found the powder, or rather the powder container and this was quite empty.

'What do we do now?' Rose wondered aloud.

Her brother, Sean, piped up, 'Look, it's only white powder. You could use flour or anything like that. That oul wig will look better no matter what powder you put on it.'

'Well, we'll try it and see. Margaret will you get out the whitest flour from Mammy's cupboard?'

She came back with two large glass jars.

'We'll take a little out of each jar, that way no one will miss it.'

They shook the white powder liberally over the old wig.

'And there's a bit for luck,' said Sean as he sprinkled on an extra handful.

The judge collected the cardboard box early next morning and after thanking everyone again and refusing to sit down for more tay he left for his court. The weather had turned very showery and it was raining heavily as he drove into his parking space which was about thirty yards from the door. He waited for a few minutes to see if the rain might stop. As he waited he opened the wig box and smiled.

'Aha, it never looked so white,' he mused.

He put on the wig and decided to make a dash for the door. By the time he locked the car and got inside the building his robes and wig were fairly wet. He was already late because of his diversion to collect the wig. He marched quickly to his bench so that the court proceedings could begin. Those of us who were present never forgot that day in court.

Back at the Deery farmhouse Rose told her mother about powdering the wig.

'Show me the powder you used,' Henrietta asked.

'Those two jars there, Mammy.'

'They're not flour, dear, they're custard powder. The flour is in the back cupboard.'

'Well, the powder is white.'

'Yes, and it will stay white until it gets wet.'

As the morning in court gathered momentum everybody found themselves staring at District Justice Raymer's head. The wig began changing colour. First of all blotches of yellow became visible. After a while the whole wig turned a deep golden yellow. The honourable judge carried on oblivious to this strange happening. Nobody dared say anything for fear of offending him. The phenomenon was causing everyone, from senior legal practitioners to simple witnesses, to lose concentration and they were unable to answer questions properly. The judge began to lose patience. Several times he admonished a speaker for dithering and being incoherent. Finally, an applicant for a bookmaker's licence was asked a question about betting odds and he kept repeating:

'I never seen the like, the odds must be a billion to one.'

Justice Raymer called a recess for half an hour. He swept into his chamber and as he passed a mirror he stopped and stared in amazement. He whipped off the wig, put it down on a chair and hurried off to get his fellow court staff. Just as he went out the door, a small pet dog belonging to the court cleaning lady spotted the wig. The little dog sniffed it and promptly began licking off the custard and in a few minutes the wig was back to its normal off-white hue. The dog's owner then appeared.

'Hm, that looks like Judge Raymer's wig.'

She picked it up, sprayed a little white talc on it and left it on the dressing table. A few minutes later the judge and half the court participants entered in a noisy throng.

'There you are,' shouted the judge, pointing at the chair, 'what do you think of that?'

They all stared at the empty chair.

'Well, it looks like a chair.' Someone proffered.

'Where's my wig gone?'

'Is this it, here on your dressing table?'

They all felt bemused. They wondered if they had imagined the wig had changed colour. The judge wondered if he was going mad. The court was due to resume. The judge then took a small whisky from a secret hiding place within his dressing table and put it to his lips. Then he stopped.

'No, maybe I'd better lay off.'

It was noticed at a parish meeting the following week that there was an unusual increase in people enquiring about taking "the pledge."

His song for the master had charm

But the missioner jumped with alarm

When Tim sang "Doris Day"

He said "stop right away

Or you'll end in a place hellish warm."

10

THE SINGER, NOT THE SONG

The headmaster from Timmy's old school had retired twenty years ago and had spent many happy and contented years since then in pursuit of his great hobby which was oil-painting. He often met Timmy while he was on his travels along the laneways and fields where he would select landscape scenes to paint. His wife had passed away five years after his retirement and they did not have any children. When he met Timmy he would raise his hat and say 'Deery, I spent the best years of my life trying to make you an academic; but look at you now; mullocking up to your arse in hay and straw.'

Timmy would look blankly at the headmaster's old hat and respond by singing:

'What is that upon your head, where did you get that bonnet?
The last time I saw one like that it had blue ribbons on it.'

They always performed this ritual when they met and the master would relate it later in the local pub to much laughter and amusement. The old master was approaching his ninety second year when he, too, passed to his eternal reward. His nephew, James, whom I knew from university, telephoned me to tell me the sad news. James told me that the family had a problem regarding instructions which the old man had left as to how his funeral service was to be conducted.

He had specified that one of his former pupils should sing solo at the church but there was only two days in which to arrange this and no suitable singer was available.

'Can you think of anyone who might fit the bill?' James asked and he sounded a bit desperate.

'I'll see what I can do,' I responded, 'but I can't guarantee anything.'

I told James that I would get back to him as soon as possible. One name kept ringing around in my head. Timmy Deery had

57

a fine baritone voice but could he be relied upon to perform at such a serious event as a funeral? I had tried every other possibility, but, due to the time restriction, with no success. So Timmy was my last resort. I found Timmy deep in manure as he cleaned out the old cow-byre. I told him about the important job that I needed someone to perform. I knew about the strained relationship between Timmy's family and the headmaster and was quite surprised by his response.

'Leave that to me,' he said.

'Do you think you will be able for it?'

'Consider it done,' he said firmly.

Nearly the whole population of the village turned out for the schoolmaster's funeral. Almost the only subject talked about after the service was Timmy Deery's singing of the hymn "Nearer My God to Thee." He sang a capella (without choral accompaniment) and all agreed that it was the most beautiful and heartfelt rendition they had ever heard.

On another occasion Timmy's singing landed him in trouble with the clergy. It happened during the parish mission. This was a major annual event which generated as much excitement as the arrival of the threshing mill. Two strange priests (missioners) would come to give the local miscreants (all males over five) a good dressing down. These grim faced men aged around sixty and with thick country accents would spread a kind of terror throughout the neighbourhood. They mostly appeared in autumn when the fields were in stubble or if the weather had been bad and the harvest was late, the uncut corn would be tinged with black and they might have a special night to pray for fine weather. The first week was for the women and regarded by some as only a warm-up for the "men's week." On this occasion a missioner was walking up Deery's lane, looking for any malefactors he might find, when he heard a loud male singing voice coming from behind the hedge.

"Che sara sara, whatever will be will be!"

Timmy was giving full voice to the new Doris Day song as he "docked" sheep in the "lane field." Suddenly this black-clad figure came through a gap in the hedge and shouted at him.

'Stop, stop, my good man, that song you are singing is blasphemous.'

Timmy let go the sheep and stood open-mouthed with shears in hand. The startled sheep shot back to her companions who were in a makeshift pen and Timmy watched in dismay as the sheep pushed against the gate which toppled over and the frightened animals ran off down the field.

'Damn, now I'll have to round them up again,' he growled. 'Who are you? You scared off the sheep.'

'Never mind the sheep, I am Fr O'Connor, your Redemptorist missioner and that song you were singing could send you to hell for all eternity. The words "whatever will be will be" are fatalistic, do you understand?'

Timmy shook his head. 'That's Doris Day's latest song, do you not like it?'

'It preaches "fatalism" and this is against church teaching, do you know what "fatalism" is?'

Timmy looked bemused.

'Flaytalism, flaytalism, would it be anything to do with "flays"? Sonny says our old dog has "flays" and he has a touch of rheumatism as well. He's going to spray him with "flay" powder.'

The veins on Fr O'Connor's red face almost burst with annoyance. He wrongly assumed that Timmy was making fun of him.

'When you come to the mission tonight I will make an example of you in front of the whole parish.' His booming voice trembled with anger.

Timmy shrugged his shoulders. 'Excuse me, father, but if I don't get these sheep back I won't have time for your mission.'

'I never met such ignorance as there is in this backwoods god-forsaken place. I'll save your soul in spite of yourself.'

The missioner sounded somewhat deflated as he hurried away, leaving a mystified Timmy to his sheep. If the good missioner thought Timmy was unusual he was soon to meet an even more out of the ordinary character. As he turned away from Deery's lane a car shuddered to a halt beside him. A genial face festooned with a black handlebar moustache and heavily brylcreamed black hair shouted out of the window.

'Can I gie ye a lift, I'm goin' te yon toon o' Roggart?'

'Oh thank you so much. I must get away from this awful godless place.'

Fr O'Connor got into the front passenger seat and was nearly knocked out by the overpowering smell of aftershave and hair oil.

'Ah ken yr a mon o th' cloth. Are ye here on yr' holliers?'

'Oh no, I'm giving a mission in St Forly's. Are you a Scotsman?'

'Hay did ye guess? Ah ma kilt gaye me awa. Ma name is Donald Dunlace, descended from the Dukes of Lammermoor and a distant relation o' Robbie Burns, the greatest poet the world has ever knane. So, yr geen a mission tae the heathens o' Roggart. Well my advice is gee them hell fire and brimstone.'

'I believe you are right, Mr Dunlace, I sometimes wonder why they go to church at all.'

'Like ma famous ancestor, I'll answer you in rhyme.'

Some gae te kirk te sigh and pray,
Some gae tae pass the time o' day,
Some gape at pictures on stained glass,
Some wink at every bonny lass.

'Here we are in Roggart, Father, where do ye want te be dropped off?'

They were coming near the Parish Church.

'This will be fine, Mr Dunlace, and thank you for such an interesting conversation.'

'May the gude laird gae wi ye, father, and don't forget, fire and brimstone.'

That evening Timmy arrived five minutes late for the mission and Fr O'Connor had already started his sermon when he spotted Timmy slipping in at the back near the choir.

'Ah, here's the man who sings modern songs,' he called out.

'Stand up, man, are you going to give us Doris Day tonight?'

'Day tonight?' Timmy repeated.

'These pop songs or whatever you call them, they undermine the faith.'

'Is it your faith you are seeking to undermine?'

'Answer up, man, what do these songs undermine?'

'Undermine?' repeated Timmy.

'Yes, undermine!'

'Under yours?' Timmy was losing track of the question.

'What's that, speak up man,'

'Is it under yours or under mine?' Timmy queried

'It's undermine.'

'What is?'

By this time the congregation was at bursting point with laughter and realizing that he was going to lose their attention completely Fr O'Connor told Timmy to resume his seat and he himself, with great difficulty, completed his sermon. On his return from the mission in Roggart Fr O'Connor surprised everyone when he resigned from his order and left to join a strictly enclosed monastery where he remained for the rest of his life.

The queen came to Roggart each year

Her kin-folk all trembled with fear

But a former old flame

So affected this dame

She still carried a torch, that was clear.

11

THE ARRIVAL OF THE QUEEN OF SHEBA

'Come out, Maloonys, she's coming, she's coming.'

Andy and Oilly Maloony were startled by loud shouting outside their house. They had just finished having their evening tea after a busy day dosing cattle. They both stopped in their tracks and their faces turned white as a sheet.

Timmy Deery's booming voice continued, 'Are yez deaf or what?, the queen is coming, the queen of Sheba, she'll be here in ten minutes, she's at the station.'

The queen referred to by Timmy was an older sister of Andy and Oilly whose name was Anne but was known as Queenie to her family and friends. Queenie had gone to England as a young girl to train as a nurse. She had been small in size and hoped to train in Ireland but the matron in the Dublin hospital said she would not be strong enough to lift and turn heavy male patients and other strenuous work which would be required. So she decided to apply for training in England where she was readily accepted and had trained and qualified to the highest level.

She had a romance going at the time with a young neighbour, Piro Callanan. She promised him faithfully that as soon as her training was finished she would come home to him and to Ireland. However, she had only been gone a few months when we heard that she had got married to a young Englishman but this had broken up after two years. They had no children and the young man had left Queenie and gone off with another woman. This was never spoken about by her brothers who were great friends with Piro.

As regards lifting heavy male patients this was no bother to Queenie, who was actually as tough as nails and was a great favourite of the male patients with whom she always exchanged lively banter, and they loved to see her in action as she reprimanded any of her fellow nurses who did not meet her high standards.

Unfortunately for Andy and Oilly she had a habit of coming back home to stay with them for a couple of weeks every year. She never gave them any prior warning of her visits and they dreaded her coming because she always did a blitzkrieg of cleaning, decorating and rearranging in the house. On a previous visit Timmy Deery had been at the bus station when she arrived and he was drafted in to carry some of her five or six pieces of luggage.

'It's like the arrival of a queen with all this bloomin' luggage,' Oilly complained.

'Maybe she is a queen.' Timmy said.

'Yeah, she's the queen of Sheba.'

From then onwards Oilly, Andy and Timmy referred to Queenie (when she was out of earshot) as the queen of Sheba.

The relaxed and lackadaisical atmosphere enjoyed by the Maloony household for eleven months of the year was suddenly shattered. She would shake their hands and hug each one at the gate, and then she would say, 'Oliver and Andrew take two cases each and deposit in my room.'

Then, sweeping into the house, she would stand with arms folded in the middle of Oilly's kitchen and give a shrill whistle through her teeth.

'What a bloomin hovel, we have an enormous task ahead of us getting this dump cleaned up. Now, will someone wet the tay?'

On this occasion she followed her usual procedure. She arrived wearing a bright red costume with tight skirt and high heeled shoes and with a figure which women half her age would die for. Timmy helped with the luggage. When they got into the kitchen Andy moved the kettle on the range to over the firebox.

Oilly said, 'I'll cut a few clipes of bread.'

'Stop, stop, the pair of you.' Queenie's voice rose to a crescendo. 'I don't believe what I'm seeing, what on God's earth is that?'

She pointed a shaking finger at a large pitchfork which she remembered being used in the cow-byre for bedding the cows with straw. It rested in a corner of the kitchen with prongs upward. Stuck on the prongs was what looked like a loaf of bread.

'Tell me I'm hallucinating.'

'What are you on about?' said Oilly. 'That's a fresh loaf I got this morning.'

'Why, oh why is it sitting up there on a blooming pitchfork?'

'Well, I just hadn't time to take it off.'

Queenie held her hands up to her head in astonishment.

'Let me get this straight, are you telling me that you carried a loaf of bread home from the shop on a pitchfork?'

'Of course, why not? Sure I had the fork with me.'

'I give up, for the moment. Come on, put on that kettle, Andy, and wet the tay, I'm famished for a cuppa.'

The kettle, which had been sitting on top of the range, was already blowing out steam and when Andy stoked the fire the extra heat soon had it boiling.

'Just give it a few minutes to draw. Oilly, will you get out the sugar and the butter and cut a few clipes of that oul loaf.

Queenie winced as Oilly wrenched the loaf off the pitchfork.

'There you are sis, a pitchfork of bread for the "lads" or a pitchfork of straw for the cows, great yoke a pitchfork.'

'Ay, that's right.' Timmy chimed in, 'I use the handle sometimes to stir the milk in the churn.'

'I don't want to hear another word about that wretched fork, just get it out of this kitchen.'

Queenie's temper was beginning to worsen. She started to pour a small amount of milk into each cup.

'What's this?' said Timmy.

'This,' said Oilly, 'is an English cup of tay. You put the milk in first and you get nothing to ate with it.'

Queenie poured a cup for herself and swept out of the kitchen.

'I'm going to my room and I'm taking my cup of tay with me. You lot can have your tay and your bread and your hay if you wish.'

When she was safely out of earshot Oilly signalled the others to gather round.

'Now, me lads,' he said quietly, 'we'll have to do something about Queenie. The last time she was here she turned this house inside out, she burned some of my best work-clothes, she made us buy carpet for the parlour, linoleum for the stairs and we had to set up that toilet yoke at the back of the pig house. I couldn't go through the like of that again.'

'But, but what can we do?' Andy spoke in a low voice.

'We'll fix her up with a fella, I know just the man.'

Oilly laughingly rubbed his hands.

'Piro Callanan!'

'But, but Piro's wife only died six months ago.'

Andy was doubtful about any scheme devised by his brother.

'Queenie was mad about Piro before she went across the water.'

'Aye but do you not remember they had a falling out and both married someone else?'

'When a man loses his wife he's always in the market for a replacement and Queenie is just the ticket.'

'Maybe, but how are you going to bring them together in such a short space of time?'

'I have an idea. Piro never learned to drive. His wife drove him everywhere and the car is still there.'

'So, maybe he doesn't want to be driven anywhere.'

'He does, he told me the other day that he desperately needs to visit his sister in Dublin and he hates the buses and Queenie is always telling us how great a driver she is. Well, now we'll give her a chance to prove it.'

'But what if the car won't start?' said Timmy. 'Or if he won't go with her?'

'It'll start. Piro always looks after things. I'll bet any money it'll start and he'll go with her, you'll see.'

'Now, Timmy, you have a role in this plan too. I want you to get over to Piro right now and tell him to be ready at nine o'clock in the morning. Meself and Andy will make sure that Queenie gets there supposing we have to carry her.'

'And now for the second part of my plan. The day that Queenie left for the nursing in England we gave her a right send-off. We had a party in the house. We roasted a pig. We ate, drank and danced. It's time we had another shindig and we'll invite Piro and all the neighbours and, me lads, we'll let nature take its course. We'll have the party ready for tomorrow night when they come back from Dublin.'

'You know, Oilly, that plan might have something going for it. What do you think, Timmy?'

'I don't remember that party. When was it?'

'You were probably not even born. It was years ago. Now will you get going and tell Piro, nine o'clock sharp and he's to come over here immediately after he gets home.'

Oilly's plan seemed to work even better than he had hoped. He told Queenie at the breakfast table that Piro was in desperate need of a driver that morning and that no one could drive in the city like she could. She seemed stunned and her eyes lit up like a teenager being asked out on a first date. She did not even tell off Andy for what she considered his obnoxious habit of slurping his tea from the saucer.

The two brothers wasted no time that day. As soon as Queenie had left, Timmy had come on his green bike and given the sign that the Queen and Piro were on the road to Dublin. Family and neighbours were drafted in and the party was organized with the same precision as the dinner at a threshing. That evening Andy and Oilly began to wonder if the main guests were going to miss their own party. Eight o'clock, nine o'clock, ten o'clock and still no sign. Finally at half past ten the old jalopy arrived and Piro jumped out of the passenger seat. He walked quickly into the house.

'Phew, I need a stiff drink after that drive.' He mopped his brow.

'What delayed you? We thought you got lost.'

'We did get lost. Everything went well until we were coming home, then we took a wrong turn somewhere and of course her ladyship "knew Dublin like the back of her hand." We drove around and around until we had to stop for petrol and then we were put on the right road.'

Piro slugged back his drink in one swallow and shrugged his shoulders, 'Ah, what the heck, life's too short for moaning; now where did Queenie get to?'

In the meantime Queenie was outside walking slowly towards the garden gate. Thirty years ago herself and Piro had stood at the same garden gate. They had looked across the yellow, purple and pink flowerbeds and lifting their eyes to the evening sky with its golden harvest moon, Piro had whispered, 'So beautiful, just like you. I could never leave this place.'

In the concrete surroundings of London Queenie's thoughts had often returned to that night and that place. The tears rolled down her cheeks. It had never changed. Not the gate, not the flowerbeds, even the moon seemed frozen in time. Then she felt an arm around her shoulders and a soft voice whispered;

'The harvest moon, so beautiful.'

Tim wanted to leave right away

And to catch a fine fish for his tay

With his rod, line and bait

The young lad could not wait

Bill landed his prize the next day

12

NEVER JUDGE A BOOK

Bill Clogher's large frame shook with laughter. He stroked his white beard, took off his horn-rimmed glasses and said in a secretive manner:

'We've hit the jackpot, Timmy lad.'

Timmy looked up from his fishing tackle box.

'Have you won on the horses Uncle Bill, what have you got there, the book of Kells or something?'

Bill's eyes gleamed as he painfully straightened his arthritic back and surveyed the contents of his late wife's old trunk which he had been clearing out. Timmy was only fifteen years old at this time and was not remotely interested in the bundle of old school books.

'Now Timothy, m'lad, I want you to help me bring these valuable books down to Jenna's shop in Roggart. I believe we're in the money.'

'But, but I'm going fishing.'

'The fish will keep, lad. If we hurry we'll get there before they shut for lunch.'

Bill Clogher was Timmy's uncle. He was regarded locally as a "gentleman" farmer. This was because he had spent his early years as a hotel barman and at around thirty years of age had taken over the small family farm in succession to his late father. Bill's wife had, sadly, passed away and as they had no family Timmy spent a lot of his time looking after the farm and just keeping the old man company. The Clogher farmhouse was about one mile from the Deery home and Timmy always enjoyed being there, mainly because Bill had a quirky sense of humour and was usually dabbling in some activity far removed from farm labouring.

'He is so fond of work that he'd lie down beside it.' A local wag unkindly observed.

A stream, which was well stocked with fish, ran along the bottom of Bill's garden and Timmy loved to fish for trout in it.

'Are you going on the bicycle or the car, Uncle Bill?'

'Well, if the automobile starts we will travel in style but if it refuses then we shall go on the old cycling machines.'

Bill's car was more than ten years old and because it was used infrequently it was difficult to start. The battery was usually low on charge. He would park the dark green Standard 8 facing down a hill and attempt to start it with a push. He would run along the driver's side with the door open, steering wheel in left hand and pushing with the right hand. When he got a bit of speed up he would jump into the driver's seat, put the car in gear and, hopefully it would start. On this occasion and with Timmy pushing as well it started first time and they roared off in a cloud of exhaust smoke.

Jenna's second-hand bookshop, a run-down red brick building on the corner of Market Lane and Main Street had not changed in forty years. It mainly covered the first floor with an overflow into the second by means of a rickety wooden staircase. As they entered through the green framed wooden door Jenna was descending the creaky stairs. In her old beige cardigan and long grey skirt she blended into the panorama of discoloured tomes reposing in equally discoloured shelving. She eyed her visitors up and down.

'What you got there, young fella?' she barked.

'Books missus,' said Timmy.

Bill interjected.

'Not just any old books, madam. These are valuable early editions of great educational value.'

Jenna flicked through the bundle of old books.

'Whouee, you could have cleaned the dust off them.'

'Naw, you could bin 'em or give them to some jumble sale or charity.'

'Come now, madam, take a closer look, see the hard covers.'

'Tell you what, for the sake of the young fella here I'll give you five bob for the lot.'

'Thanks, missus,' said Timmy, 'Come on Uncle Bill, take the money and we'll head for home.'

Bill Clogher had no intention of going without a haggle over the old books. As the haggling continued, Timmy began to root around at the back of the shop.

'Phew, this place smells of old boots,' he muttered. 'Attishoo!'

The dusty old books made Timmy sneeze and sneeze.

'Hey, Uncle Bill, are you near finished? I want to go home,' he shouted in between sneezes.

After a particularly loud sneeze, Timmy tripped over a torn carpet and knocked over a pile of books at the side of the stairs. This started a chain reaction and the books which lined the banisters cascaded to the floor in an untidy heap.

'What's that young lad doing out there?' shrieked Jenna.

'Nuttin,' missus, I'm just tidying the shop for you.'

Timmy shoved the heap of books under the stairs and out of sight. He started sneezing again.

'Uncle Bill, are you coming?'

Bill stayed put. He had got the price up to six shillings.

'This calls for drastic action,' Timmy murmured to himself.

He remembered seeing a film with strange horrible worms crawling around and scaring the life out of people and this gave him an idea. He took from his pocket the box of fishing bait he had gathered in the garden that morning. It was full of live maggots. From another pocket he took a small plastic bag of flour (also part of his fishing stuff). He sprinkled flour until the maggots were a wriggling white mass. Then, opening a large flat book, he emptied the maggots onto it and rushing out to Jenna he shouted.

'Hey missus, missus, the worms are eating your books. Look, look.'

Jenna screamed. 'Get that dirt out of here immediately.'

Timmy quickly emptied the maggots back into his box and shoved it into his pocket.

Bill (who was used to his nephew's antics) said, 'Tut tut, Timothy lad, this won't do at all.'

Jenna chased both of them out and Bill found himself having to come back next day to apologize and to collect his old school books. But he had another surprise. Jenna had looked through the books and had found an old single pound note inserted between the pages of one.

'Madame Jenna,' said Bill, in his most beguiling manner, 'will you do me the honour of helping me to spend this unexpected windfall?'

Bill and Jenna's was the first wedding that Timmy ever attended. He sat at the top table.

City folk came to holiday with joy

Amid meadows they ate rabbit pie

But their humour soon dropped

In the doghouse they flopped

It's best to let sleeping dogs lie.

13

HOLIDAYS WITH TAY

The Swandleys came to Roggart during the very hot summer of fifty four. They arrived in a maroon-coloured Ford van which was towing a blue and white caravan. They said they were city people but this was debated by the locals. They rolled into the Deery farmyard one evening in late July and asked Sonny, who was tidying up, if they could have a drink of water. They explained that they were on holidays for two weeks and wanted to stay in the countryside. They were a cheerful group numbering about seven or eight and ranging in age from baby to sixtyish. The most senior male figure got out of the van, looked around and observed, 'Is dere many rabbits around here?'

'The place is full of them, they're a bloomin' pest,' said Sonny.

'Dat field dere would be ideal, mister, do you tink we could stay dere for a few days, we wouldn't be any truble an we'd pay you mister?'

Sonny agreed and the first year's Swandley summer fortnight passed off without much incident. They were a source of amusement to the locals as they always went out in the early hours of the morning and came back laden with rabbits which they skinned, cooked and ate, around an outdoor fire. The womenfolk called several times a day to Sonny's wife, Henrietta, to borrow a grain of tay or sugar. They also came again the next year, with the same van and caravan, and their numbers had increased to about a dozen. The Deerys and other locals got to know several of the Swandleys by name.

There was the family patriarch, Peter "Snare" Swandley and his wife, Grainne, and their family of three boys, Bartler, a dapper "ladies" man, Robert known as "Razor" and the youngest boy, Eammo, who was twelve years old. There were four girls, three of whom were married with babies. The eldest girl, Grace, was single. She was tall and rangy and the men all agreed she was the best rabbit catcher in the family. Her ears stuck out prominently and they said she took size ten boots. She became very friendly with Henrietta and confided to her that she had wanted to be a nun when she left school, but her ma and da had soon put a stop to that idea. She now worked in a toy shop near her home.

The second year's holiday was a bit more controversial among the locals. The Swandley area of operation widened outward as they foraged for food. Potatoes, turnips and rabbits were their most preferred foods. One evening Ivor Nale returned from work and came across Bartler digging potatoes in his garden. Ivor walked quietly up behind him and then said in a loud voice,

'Well, Bartler, do you think are they fit enough to come out yet?'

A startled Bartler turned around.

'Well, dey're nearly dere, sir, dey might be better in another week or so, I was just going to pay for dese few I was diggin' for de childers' dinner. Be gob we Swandleys always pay our way. How much do I owe you sir?'

'You can have those for the childer, but next time go to the greengrocer, you'll find he's cheaper than me.'

The third year the Swandleys again arrived on cue as July was drawing to a close and this time their population showed a definite increase and two caravans were dragged into the Deery field. They had always had a few dogs, mainly small terriers for hunting rabbits, but now they had five or six large wolf-like Alsatians. The locals viewed these with alarm. Rumours gradually spread around the village about sheep being chased and killed, about young children being scared to pass by the Deery farmhouse and about cyclists being chased on the road. Although these were unproven and simply rumours, the result was that a deputation of Roggart parents came to Sonny and asked him to remove the holiday-makers at once, before something serious occurred.

Sonny went into the caravan field and sought out the leader, "Snare." He told him that one week was all they could stay for this year and, unfortunately, the field would not be available next year as he was going to plough it for a crop of wheat.

"Snare" had heard the rumours about the dogs and was not surprised by this. However, the "guard dogs" as he called them belonged to one of the new arrivals named Georgie who happened to be married to his youngest daughter. Georgie's business was in "security." He supplied guard dogs on hire to people who required them. He trained the dogs himself and out in the Meath countryside was an ideal place for this with no interference from the law or any other busybodies. Georgie had a reputation of not being a man to meddle with.

'Mr Deery,' said "Snare," 'do you not think you could leave us for the two weeks this year and we'll go somewhere else next year?'

'I don't think that—' Sonny's reply was interrupted by a chilling low almost whisper from Georgie, who had been listening in the background.

'Listen up, farmer, city people are entitled to spend a couple of weeks out here if they want to and we're staying.'

'Oh, yeah, who says so?'

'Me and me pal here, "Hungry Wolf," we kinda like it out here.'

Georgie held a struggling Alsatian dog by his stout leather collar. 'How'd you like a nip on the ass from old Wolfie?'

Sonny looked around to see that he was encircled by the entire Swandley clan.

'Ok,' he said, 'I get the message, but you may be sorry,'

Sonny turned and walked away, the circle of Swandleys opening up a gap to let him through. As he cleared the circle there was a loud cheering augmented by the barking of the dogs. Shouts of "yella," "up the Swandleys," "not an inch, boys" rang out in his wake as he walked to the house. When word of this episode got around there was much foreboding among the local residents and three days later another confrontation took place.

Timmy Deery was returning alone from leaving cows in the top field when he suddenly walked into a crowd of Swandley men in an adjoining field "training" their dogs. The large wolf-like animals were being taught to attack dummy forms of human figures made from old clothes and rags. When Timmy came on the scene, they all stopped and stared at him. Then Georgie, who was holding "Wolfie" shouted out.

'Just stay right there Mr D. We were letting them play with dummies but "Wolfie" here prefers real dummies.'

The creature's yellow eyes shone like a lazar and he howled as his dribbling tongue hung out over teeth as sharp as the glistening icicles that Timmy had once seen in an underground cave. Georgie set him loose.

'Go get him boy!'

As the large snarling animal bounded forward Timmy stood for a second, then he amazed the onlookers by moving towards the dog. Dropping on one knee and holding out his hand he said softly.

'At a boy, come here boy, come to your uncle Timmy, boy.'

The wolf-like creature stopped in his tracks. He sidled shyly up to Timmy and almost licked his outstretched hand, then with his tail between his legs he trudged back to where he started from while the other dogs whined. Timmy stood up but said nothing. The Swandleys also were silent and then they moved slowly away. The next morning the old van and both caravans had disappeared as had the whole Swandley entourage along with their pack of dogs. They never came back to Roggart again.

A coloured pullover so quaint

That his mother could knit like a saint

Mickey Joe couldn't bear it

T'would kill him to wear it

Today's style and fashion it aint

14

KNIT NO MORE MOTHER DEAR

Dolores Mayfel shot to a kind of local fame suddenly and unexpectedly. She was a lady whose appearance never seemed to change over the years. She was small, about five foot two, with brownish hair which she usually wore in a bun, and had a round smiling face and big blue eyes. She was definitely middle aged but a young looking middle age. This made her attractive in an odd sort of way to men with a wide spread of ages.

Those in their twenties laughed and chatted and looked completely at ease in her company. Men in their thirties and forties always regarded her as belonging to their own age group and, of course, with these she was decidedly popular. Those of fifty, sixty and older ages could happily converse with her on subjects from their own interest sphere and she could equally match them in all topics. Dolores was a single lady and all in Roggart were at a loss to know why, because she was a wonderful worker, intelligent, but a bit dumb as well, which was an almost perfect combination in any person, male or female. She was not particularly well educated and did not pretend that she knew anything about politics or higher mathematics. In other words she never posed a threat to those who had an inflated opinion of themselves. Everybody, and I really mean everybody, was comfortable in her company and this may be the reason, or part of the reason, for her eventual status as a much sought after adviser, especially by young men with anxieties or worries.

Kathleen O'Grady had been widowed after only five years of marriage. She was much admired for the single-handed rearing of two girls and one boy. The boy's name was Mickey Joe. He was now about thirty years old and was regarded as a moody individual. When he was five Kathleen entered a "Smiley Suds" knitting competition. She knitted a brightly coloured fairisle sleeveless pullover which the young Mickey Joe modelled for the judges in the Faz factory in Dublin and her prize for winning was a year's supply of Faz washing powder. The proud mother and toddler's photograph appeared in all the newspapers and from this time onward Kathleen never stopped knitting these same garments, and Mickey Joe never stopped wearing these fairisle pullovers. Every colour of the rainbow was used in their creation, reds, blues, yellows, greens. Neighbours gave her their surplus bits of wool and all Mickey Joe's complaints and hints of his dislike of the garments were ignored.

And now at thirty years of age Mickey Joe was asked by his mother to model a pullover again at the Roggart Women's Sewing Circle meeting, where she was giving a knitting demonstration. The unfortunate man went into a black depression and said he would rather throw himself under a bus or maybe a train. Kathleen as usual ignored him and said 'Don't fret, love, you'll be a great hit on the night.'

But this time Mickey Joe was intent on showing that he had reached the end of his tether and that he had to protest with some striking gesture which could not be ignored. In The Cozy Bar he tried telling a few men of his own age what he was going to do but they just laughed and started talking about football. The city bus came each evening at seven o'clock and stopped outside Murphy's Garage. Mickey Joe wandered down towards the garage and felt really good. He would show them once and for all. He came to a bend in the road where a tree half hid him from the oncoming bus and as he leaned out to see if it was coming down the road, he noticed that there was a car in front of the bus. Sitting in the passenger seat was Dolores Mayfel who waved as she passed.

Mickey Joe swore and jumped back into the ditch as the bus sped past.

'Feck it, that was a close one, Dolores nearly caught me,' he muttered, 'I'll have to plan this more carefully.'

He was walking back towards his home when, suddenly, Dolores stepped out from a side road and walked along with him.

'How is it going, Mickey, how is life treating you?' she said in her usual cheery manner.

'Well to tell you the truth, Dolores, if mother doesn't stop knitting fairisle pullovers for me, I'm going to throw myself in front of a bus, or maybe a train.'

'Will you don't be such an eejit,' she retorted, 'I'll make you an offer, I'll knit you an Aran sweater and I'll swop it with you for the fairisle pullover.'

Well, Mickey Joe felt ten feet tall.

'Dolores is knitting me an Aran sweater,' he delightedly told everyone he met.

True to her word, two weeks later, Dolores posted a note to Mickey Joe (another boost for him) telling him to come down to the house (yet another boost) and collect the Aran sweater. There was a further triumph at Mass on the following Sunday when Dolores wore the large fairisle pullover like a mini dress. Mickey Joe's mother was livid when she saw her.

'Who do you think you are?' she snapped at Dolores on their way out of the church after Mass.

'You look ridiculous in that outfit, that pullover was specially knitted for my son and not for some fancy dress parade.'

Dolores simply said 'and a good morning to you too, Kathleen,' and quietly went on her way.

This event started a kind of craze among the younger women and they began asking Mickey Joe if he would sell them some of his pullovers because they all knew that he had a huge collection as his mother knitted several every year. And Mickey Joe wooed one particular girl by giving her a present of seven fairisle pullovers, one for every day of the week. On their wedding day he wore a dress suit and his bride wore a long white dress.

Dolores was credited with lifting Mickey Joe out of his depression and from this time onward many people sought her advice and she always had time to listen no matter how trivial the matter was. This also led to her own special romance, but that's a story for another day.

The man said this is such a dull place

Not another day here could he face

Trains, zebras nor cattle

Nor cowboy gun battle

Could deter him from packing his case.

15

WAITING FOR A TRAIN

It was a showery evening in late September and Timmy Deery was nearing the end of a ten mile long cattle drive from his home farm to the outskirts of Roggart town. He was delivering seven fat cattle to a dealer who exported them by boat to England "on the hoof." He walked all the way with the cattle on what was a fairly quiet road and with about one mile to go he noticed that his herd had increased to eight animals. They had been joined by a stray donkey and Timmy observed that it was a rather old female donkey, the kind which was frequently abandoned by a careless owner and left to fend for itself. He was a bit annoyed because this made the drive more difficult but he decided to allow the donkey to accompany the cattle and when he reached his destination he hoped there would be a solution and that some kind of home could be found for it. Timmy himself intended coming home on the one bus which departed from the nearby railway station and this is why he walked with the cattle rather than bring his green bicycle. The station was near to the dealer's holding pen into which he would put the cattle.

When he reached the pen there were two men waiting to receive the cattle. The donkey brayed loudly when she saw them and ran away from the men who promptly picked up handfuls of stones and uttering loud expletives they threw the stones at the fleeing animal.

'What did the poor old donkey do to deserve that treatment?' said Timmy.

'He's only an ass and I don't like asses much.'

Timmy knew there was no chance of a home for the donkey there, so he finished delivering the seven cattle and made his way to the railway station terminal where he would get the bus for home. Dressed in his old farm working clothes and faded check cap he cut a rather shabby figure at the almost deserted station. Another man dressed in a navy suit which had seen better days and carrying a battered brown suitcase also was waiting. He nodded at Timmy.

'You waiting for the train?'

'No,' replied Timmy, 'I'm waiting for the bus.'

'Well, you're always waiting for something in a back-of-the-woods place like this, waiting for something to happen and it never does.'

The man sat down on the iron bench seat while Timmy walked along the platform looking at an empty train which stood silent and waiting.

'Aye, we're all waiting, maybe that man is right,' Timmy thought.

The front carriages, which had number 1 on the doors, were furnished with shiny green leather seats and he gazed in wonder at their opulence. As he moved along towards the rear carriages, with number 2 on the door, the green leather was replaced by rough wooden seats and as Timmy gazed intensely through the dust laden windows he could just about make out the green fields on the far side of the track.

Then he was distracted by what he thought was somebody moving inside the carriage. 'Maybe there's someone hiding in there,' he thought.

He walked back to the seat and noticed that the man in the navy suit had gone and there was just an old newspaper lying on the seat. He sat down and took up the newspaper. The headlines read

"Prisoner escapes from jail, police hunt for gunman,"

"Dangerous wild zebra escapes from travelling circus and zoo."

Timmy got a fright.

'The man in the carriage,' he thought, 'He could be the gunman.'

He crept around behind a concrete wall and looked at the carriage and then his worst fears seemed to be confirmed. The man had a bag on his back and sticking out of it Timmy saw the shape of a gun handle. He looked around hoping to see the man in the navy suit but there was no sign of him. He stared at the carriage and strained his eyes to try to identify what was going on. The man seemed to be just sitting down waiting. Looking right through the windows of the carriage Timmy made out the shape of a donkey in the field at the other side of the tracks. Or was it a donkey at all? The dirty windows made it almost impossible to be certain, but the animal figure seemed to have vertical stripes, or was that just the dirt on the glass?

While Timmy was engrossed with the carriage figure and the animal, the station was beginning to come to life. Four or five men arrived on bicycles. They wore the grubby dark blue rail company uniform. One had a peaked cap and he walked along the platform in a superior manner. As he passed the seat on which Timmy was sitting he said loudly and without looking at anyone in particular,

'Passengers get your tickets from the ticket office, platform tickets are required for others who wish to use the platform.'

'Have you got your ticket young fellow?'

'Just going to get it,' said Timmy.

As he walked out of the station to the nearby bus stop Timmy noticed that more and more people were arriving and the train which was silent was making strange bursts of noise as it blew off steam and warmed up for its upcoming journey. The clock over the station door told Timmy that he had another twenty minutes to wait for the bus. He wondered what to do about the man in the carriage. He still held the paper in his hand. He wished there was a policeman around. He had reservations about informing the railway guard because on a previous occasion he had not been believed when he had attempted to tell a bus conductor that his bus was on fire.

He had seen numerous films about trains. In fact only last week The Lone Ranger had jumped from his horse, Silver, on to the roof of a speeding train, swung himself in through a window and captured a notorious outlaw.

'Why not, if he can do it on a speeding train then I can surely do it on a train that's stopped.'

Timmy's imagination went into overdrive. He slipped back into the station, hiding behind pillars and in doorways until he reached the carriage where the man was. To his annoyance the carriage was now half full of people and the platform guard had his flag ready to send the train on its way. The man with the back pack was standing up and seemed to be arguing with a boy passenger of about ten years of age.

'But dad, we live in Meath now, they don't play much hurling up here,' the boy was arguing.

Then to Timmy's horror the man opened the bag and was about to draw out the gun. At this point things happened so quickly that there was confusion all round. Timmy sprang forward and grabbed at the bag.

'Drop it you pesky outlaw or I'll blow you to kingdom come,' he shouted.

The poor man was dumbstruck. He dropped the bag and the contents scattered around the floor of the train. Among the items was a hurling stick and a blue and gold coloured Tipperary jersey. The man had bought these for his son but the young lad really wanted a football. This was what Timmy mistook for a gun.

'What's going on here?'

The voice was that of the train ticket inspector. Timmy quickly recovered his composure.

'I made a mistake, I'm sorry Mr, eh, eh, what's your name?'

'Joe Ryan, but, but.'

'I'll make it up to you, have to fly—'

Timmy jumped out the door while the startled passengers and ticket inspector gazed after him. He raced over to the far side of the track and ducked down behind a clump of furze bushes.

After what seemed like an eternity the train moved off and Timmy breathed a sigh of relief. Then he got another surprise. Something pushed him from behind. It was the old donkey that had joined him on the cattle drive.

'Something looks different about you, old girl. You look as though someone tried to paint white stripes on your coat.'

The rain had washed some of the paint off and left a kind of silver colour behind.

'You look more silvery, I know we'll call you "Silver," hey, Silver, here comes the bus. I'm afraid this is where we say goodbye.'

Two days later Timmy was cycling to the pictures in Roggart and, as usual, he sang a song as he rode along the road. As he came to a little wood at about half way he stopped suddenly.

'I think I heard a moaning sound in that little wood,' he muttered.

On investigation he found an old donkey lying on the ground and obviously in trouble. The creature had got a severe wetting from heavy rain the previous day and Timmy knew that a donkey's coat, unlike that of other animals, was not waterproof. He had to act fast and get the animal dried out and warmed up. This was one of the few times that the cinema was not Timmy's first priority. He cycled home and told his brother, Sonny, how urgent the situation was. Sonny drove the tractor with Timmy perched behind on the trailer, sitting on a bale of dry straw and holding a can of warm drinking water for the donkey. Silver the donkey (yes, it was Silver) became part of the Deery farm family.

A few days later Timmy found out where Joe Ryan lived. He cycled to the house and delivered a package with his apologies. Joe's young son, who had recovered from the dramatic incident on the train, could hardly believe it. The package was for him and contained a football and two football jerseys (one in the Meath green and gold colours and the other in the blue and gold of Tipperary). Mrs Ryan, with much laughter at the story, wet the tay for their visitor. The Ryans told how they had come from their native Tipperary twelve years ago to live in Meath. Joe was a hurling man and hoped that his sons would carry on this tradition, but he laughingly accepted that they would probably become Meath footballers. They all came out to the gate to say goodbye to Timmy and just then a man in a navy suit and carrying a brown suitcase walked past. It was the same man that Timmy had met waiting at the station.

'Good evening, all,' he said in a rather dreary voice. 'Sure it's a miserable day, nothing ever happens in this back-of-beyond. We'd all be better off out of here.'

Timmy Deery at last found his feet

But with no shoes there wasn't much heat

Strange sounds in the night

Made him shiver with fright

Said Joe "You're a hard man to beat"

16

ON THE OTHER FOOT

It was a cold winter's evening. The residue of snow which had fallen one week previously still lay along the shady side of the thorn hedge as Timmy Deery carried the newly born calf in his arms, while the calf's mother followed along about three yards behind. The cow cried out from time to time in a plaintive manner. Timmy placed the calf in the small shed which he had previously bedded with fresh straw and closed and bolted the door before the calf's distraught mother could enter. He did not like having to separate them but that was the way that dairy farmers who produced milk for sale worked. If the calf was left to suckle the cow there would be no milk to sell, so the calf had to be fed by other means.

He then steered the cow into the main byre where he tethered her with the cow chain, got his milking stool and bucket and hand-milked her. Then he fed the new calf with the fresh beiscins.

By this time darkness was falling and Timmy finished up his farmyard chores and went into the house. Later that night he awoke to the sound of what he imagined must be a ghost. It was a strange screeching noise and seemed to be coming from outside in the farmyard. Then the noise suddenly stopped and Timmy lay down and settled back to sleep. He had scarcely closed his eyes when the noise started up again. This time the screeching seemed nearer and louder and to be right underneath his window. Although he was scared by the strange sound he, nevertheless, crawled out of bed and over to the window to see what was causing this. Peering through the frosted glass he could just barely make out the shape of two cats fighting.

'I'll soon put a stop to this racket,' Timmy muttered.

Then, taking a shoe in one hand, he opened the window with the other and let fly. The shoe missed by a considerable distance.

Timmy threw another shoe, and then another and another until, at last, "bingo," one of the shoes hit a tomcat on the ear and they both slunk away into the night. Timmy closed the window and went back to bed. Nobody else in the house was woken. The next morning Timmy dressed and then discovered that all his footwear was missing. Then he remembered the tomcats and the shoes and boots which he had thrown out the window.

'Drat, what am I going to do now?' he muttered, as he looked out on the frosty cold yard.

'Maybe, I could lift a pair of boots or shoes with my fishing rod and line.'

He made a hook from a piece of fencing wire that he had in his pocket, tied it to the line and proceeded to "fish" for a shoe. He was sitting propped up against the side of the open window when he heard a rattling sound coming up the lane.

'Oh, it's only the milk lorry,' he thought.

The milk-stand where the lorry stopped was in full view of Timmy's window. Joe, the driver, gazed up at the figure silhouetted against the morning light in amazement.

'Did you catch many this morning? Mr D,' he shouted up at Timmy.

'No, you're the first,' replied Timmy.

Joe laughed. 'Very droll, Mr D, very droll.'

'Could you throw me up a pair of those shoes, please?' Timmy said.

Joe tossed up two shoes which Timmy caught and attempted to put on.

'No, these are not a pair, throw up a few more.'

Joe, who was a stocky rotund man dressed in a brown overall, shook with laughter as he threw the shoes and boots in Timmy's direction. Timmy failed to catch some of these and they fell down again. After a while Joe began to lose patience as he hated being delayed on his milk collection round. He thought he had found the last pair of shoes and quickly turned around to throw when he slipped on the frosty ground and the shoe went sailing through the air just as Sonny, who had been having breakfast with Henrietta in the kitchen, opened the door to come outside. The shoe whizzed past his ear and landed in a sugar bowl right on the kitchen table. A startled Sonny quickly shut the door.

'We're being attacked,' he shouted.

Henrietta, meanwhile, had gone to call the children to get up for school. She quickly ran back to see what Sonny was shouting about.

'Sonny, what's going on?'

'I don't know, but somebody threw a missile at me when I opened the door. There's something strange going on outside.'

Meanwhile, Joe had quickly loaded the cans of milk on to his lorry, unloaded the empties and driven away, forgetting that he had slipped the last shoe into his coat pocket. When he felt the shoe he quickly tossed it out the window of the lorry where it was immediately picked up by Towser, the family dog, which had followed the lorry as it sped off.

'It seems quiet out there now,' Sonny muttered, 'I'd better go out and take a look around.'

'Be careful.'

Out in the yard Sonny scratched his head as he watched the familiar sight of the milk lorry rattling away in the distance. Timmy had silently disappeared inside and closed the window.

'Well that beats Banagher.'

Towser, the dog, then appeared with a shoe in his mouth, which his sharp teeth had chewed into an unrecognizable shape. Henrietta was standing at the door and she had picked up the shoe which had landed on the kitchen table.

'I think this looks like Timmy's shoe,' she said.

Timmy then appeared behind her. 'What's going on; is that my shoe you have there?'

'Yes, it looks like yours, but how did it arrive at the kitchen table?'

'Well don't look at me,' Timmy retorted. 'Towser must have brought it in. I'm going to milk the cows.'

Timmy brushed passed and walked towards the cow-byre. The children had come out and were laughing as they watched their uncle's peculiar gait. Timmy was wearing a shoe on one foot and a wellington boot on the other.

Sonny and Henrietta broke into wide smiles as he disappeared into the cow-byre.

Henrietta said laughingly, 'Yes, Timmy, this time you really put your foot in it. But it's a cold morning, so come inside for a bit of heat everyone, the tay is wet.'

GLOSSARY
of Terms used

BANJAXED, *Broken, ruined*

BEISCINS. *Milk from a freshly calved cow*

BOCKETY. *Uneven, crudely built*

BUCK LEP. *A sudden wild jump*

CLIPE. *Thick slice (of bread)*

DOCK SHEEP. *Cut off soiled wool from tail of sheep*

ELDER. *Udder*

FLAYS. *Fleas*

FURZE. *Gorse*

GESHEH. *Young girl*

HAGGARD. *Area at back of farmyard for storing hay and straw.*

HAY SLIDE. *A two wheel low flat cart or bogey.*

MULLOCK. *Do heavy manual work*

PIKE. *A stack or rick (of hay)*

PITCH & TOSS. *A gambling game played with coins by men (usually on the public road)*

PLEDGE. Promise to abstain from drinking alcohol.

STRIG. Take the last drop of milk from cow.

STROP. A flexible piece of leather with gritted sharpening surface.

STUCK, To stand about ten sheaves of corn together and tie two sheaves on top.

TAY. Tea

WET THE TAY. Pour boiling water onto tea in teapot

WINNOWING MACHINE. For cleaning corn after flail threshing. Used in pre threshing mill days.

THE AUTHOR

Ben Ryan was born and reared on a small dairy farm near Duleek, Co Meath. His brothers farmed while he worked in industry. Now retired, his consuming leisure enjoyments are writing, painting and music.

His grounding in these pursuits goes back to the 'seventies' with his involvement in the local Ardcath variety group. Script writing, painting scenery, arranging musical scenes, were all combined in successful Pioneer and Tops of the Town stage shows.

He is involved in Duleek local heritage and history and has a BA in history and economics from University College Dublin. The social scene portrayed is firmly based on his memories of life and events in rural Meath in the middle of the last century. Each chapter is introduced by an amusing limerick, and the characters are portrayed sympathetically and with great humour.